CAFE NOIRE
A Beest & Beauty Tale

Airship 27 Productions

TM

Cape Noire: A Beest & Beauty Tale
©2022 Ron Fortier

Brother Bones, Cape Noire and its denizens are © and ™ Ron Fortier

An Airship 27 Production
airship27.com
airship27hangar.com

Cover and interior illustrations © 2022 Rob Davis

Editor: Ron Fortier
Associate Editor, Art Director and Designer: Rob Davis
Promotion and Marketing Manager: Michael Vance

ISBN: 978-1-953589-19-4

Printed in the United States of America

10 9 8 7 6 5 4 3 2 1

CAFE NOIRE
A Beest & Beauty Tale

by Ron Fortier

CHAPTER (1)

The left hook caught Butch Hammer on the jaw and knocked him back. He shook his head to clear it while bringing up his arms to block Slammer Morgan's follow up strikes. Punch after punch hit Hammer's forearms leaving him no time to react or counter. Morgan had the longer arms and it was obvious he was going to beat Hammer while staying out of range.

Hammer blinked, and biting down on his mouth guard, barreled forward into those beating fists. Any fight strategy he remembered had been beaten out of him in the last six rounds and now all he wanted to do was get some pay-back. If it meant he had to take a couple of hard shots to his shoulders and arms, so be it. But he had to push the big guy to the center of the ring where he could finally do some of his own damage.

The crowd was roaring as he managed to finally drive his opponent back and off balance. For all his strength, Slammer Morgan was flatfooted and having to back pedal wobbled his balance for a second. In that moment, his arms dropped and Hammer stepped in fast, his own fists pounding away. He centered his blows to Morgan's stomach, each hitting with the force of a machine piston.

Caught off guard, Slammer Morgan continued to retreat until his back was against the ropes. Now it was his turn to try and protect himself from Hammer's relentless punishment. The tall fighter's hands began to fall again. It was the opening Hammer was looking for. He attacked his face mercilessly until blood appeared from Morgan's nose and over his left eye.

"Enough," the referee yelled, grabbing Hammer's right shoulder. "Back off!"

But Hammer was lost in his own all-consuming rage and nothing else mattered except for beating the big man to a pulp. Again the ref tried to pull him away, but Hammer turned and backhanded him across the face. The referee fell to the canvas senseless allowing the maddened fighter to continue his brutal onslaught.

Within minutes, Slammer Morgan was standing senseless held up only by the black ring chords pressing against his back. Then he merely slid down and fell to the mat where he lay unmoving.

Though the haze of his uncontrolled fury, Hammer made out others now in the ring, some kneeling over Morgan while his own people were pulling him away.

What had he done? Where was he? Who was that on the mat?

One of Morgan's corner men, a towel draped around his neck, kneeling beside the motionless boxer, looked up at Hammer. His eyes were wide with disbelief as he cried out, "He's dead! You killed him!"

What? He wasn't hearing right. *He can't be dead!*

In his dazed confusion, Hammer saw the ring was now filled with lots of other people. As if the spectators had climbed over the ropes and were now starting to surround him. In front of them was a harried woman he recognized only from pictures he'd seen in the newspapers.

"You killed my husband," Bertha Morgan screamed pointing a finger at him. "What am I going to tell our three kids? How are we going to survive without him?"

"I'm sorry," Hammer sputtered, holding out his gloved hands only to see they were covered by bright red blood. It was so thick, it splattered to the floor.

"Blood on your hands!" the woman cried all the louder. "BLOOD ON YOUR HANDS."

A hand grabbed Butch Hammer's left shoulder and he yelled. "Aaghhh!"

"Hey, wake up, mister," the anxious voice said.

Hammer sat up straight, his eyes opening to the train car and the motion of the steel wheels beneath them. It was dark except for a few overhead lights now dimmed to allow passengers to sleep; if they could.

The concerned black conductor released his hold on Hammer's shoulder. "You was having a bad dream, mister. Is all."

"Right," the former boxer conceded, running a hand through his sandy colored hair. "I'm sorry."

"No need," the conductor smiled showing off perfect white teeth. "We all get the night jitters every now and then."

Hammer looked around. A few of the other travelers, obviously awakened by his shouts, were now attempting to get back to sleep; some clearly annoyed.

"Thank you. How soon before we reach Cape Noire?"

"We's on schedule, sir. Should roll into the station a few hours from now. Just about sunup. You sure I can't get you something from the club car? Maybe a drink to settle your nerves."

"No. I'm fine now. Really. Thanks for waking me."

"Just doing my job." The friendly trainman tipped his cap and walked off.

Hammer sighed and leaned his head back on the seat. He was seated next to the window and looking out at the night landscape. He looked at his own reflection in the glass. His face, with its rough square jaw and pug nose looked a lot older than his thirty years. *That's what killing a man will do your soul,* he thought. He hadn't had that dream in weeks. He sighed. Even leaving Trenton, New Jersey behind and traveling across the entire country wouldn't ever make him totally free.

That peace might elude him the rest of his life. He prayed it would not be the case and sighed deeply as he closed his eyes. But this time only to rest them. He had no intention of going back to sleep.

It was shortly after six-thirty in the morning when the Great Northern Flier pulled into Station Central depot at the center of the Brickyard; a fifty acre railyard located just northeast of Cape Noire's downtown. From this transportation nexus, both passenger and freight trains travel south along the Pacific coast for warmer climes found in California to points northward into rugged Canada and beyond that Alaska.

With a long blast of its whistle and a volcano like puff of hot white smoke from its engine stack, the coal black iron horse came to a screeching stop in front of the long, rectangular green wooden station house.

Bradley "Butch" Hammer was among the passengers who climbed down onto the open platform covered over by a long overhanging portico. Crisp, cold air greeted him as he made his way through the growing cluster of people, porters, and various reception committees awaiting loved ones. He made his way through the main lobby of the station and was pleased to see it had a cafeteria area open for business and serving breakfast. He got in the short line, put in an order of coffee, bacon and eggs with toast and then preceded down the aisle to the register where a tired looking woman with a cigarette hanging from her thin lips was taking payment.

As Hammer handed her a buck, one of the two short-order chefs working the grill pushed his plate of food across the counter at him.

"I ordered a coffee too," he said, as the clerk handed him change.

She pointed to the small table against the wall on which were set two huge coffee machines and stacks of white porcelain mugs. There were several creamers and a bowl of filled with sugar cubes.

Hammer set down his tray of food, prepared a cup of joe with two sugars then set it on the tray. Carefully he moved to one of a half dozen small round tables. After setting down his tray, he dropped his canvas back-pack to the floor, pulled out one of the two wooden chairs and sat. He took a long sip of coffee. It was passable. He'd had worse. Just the fact that it was hot was all he required. He took another sip, then picked up his fork and began to chow down on his first meal in what he hoped would be his new home for some time to come.

After finishing his breakfast, Hammer lit up a cigarette, grabbed his kit and exited through the terminal's front entrance. Bright sunlight cast the busy street before him in harsh colors as buses, taxis, and private vehicles arrived and departed the circular drive that fronted the massive station. The noise of honking horns and shouting voices added to the scene as people of all shapes and sizes, races and colors, poor and well-to-do of all ages came and went all around him testifying to this hellhole of humanity that was called Cape Noire.

He blew out a puff a smoke and approached a chubby porter who had just helped a fancy looking dame into a yellow cab.

"Which bus to downtown?" he asked the station employee busy stuffing a dollar tip into his jacket.

The porter turned his head surveying the busy sidewalk lane and pointed to his left. "That second bus in line," he indicated. "Number Eight will take you to Central Ave. Pretty much the heart of the city."

Hammer reached into his pants pocket, fished out a quarter and flipped it to the man. "Thanks." He made his way to the designated bus where several people were filing in and he joined them. As he came up the interior steps, he saw the card sign taped over a small bucket indicating the cost of a nickel. Once again he dug into his change and withdrew the Indian Head coin and dropped it in the bucket.

The bus was almost full as he made his way to a vacant aisle seat near the middle. Occupying the window half of the padded seat was an old woman with a plaid kerchief tied around her face and a worn travel bag on her lap. Hammer nodded to her, dropped into the seat, and like her, put his own kit on his lap.

Seeing the bus was full up, the driver closed the accordion doors, put the bus in gear and then turning the wheel started into the street, carefully avoiding any passing cars.

Hammer took a final drag on his cigarette, dropped it to the floor and crushed it out with the toe of his shoe. Then he sat back and watched the city roll by.

CHAPTER (2)

"I'm hungry," thirteen year old Tommy Bonello told his twin brother Jack.

"Me too," Jack added, punching Tommy on the arm as they walked along Thatcher St.

The boys were identical in every way; from their rugged, dark good looks to their tall, lean bodies dressed in soiled jeans, ripped canvas shoes, and thick, coarse sweaters they'd snatched off a neighborhood clothesline a few days earlier. With the harbor district just several blocks away, the clothing did little to protect them from the morning's bracing cold wind.

"How about Delmont's Bakery?" Tommy suggested, brushing back his greasy, thick black hair. "We can grab some donuts and be out of there before the old coot knows what hit him."

"Yeah, sounds good to me," Jack, who was older by two minutes, replied. "They're great when fresh baked. Let's go."

Without another word, the boys started racing down the sidewalk with no concern for the pedestrians they scattered along the way. They were known around the block and people in the area did their best to avoid them. The Bone Brothers, as they had been tagged, were nothing but trouble from the day they were born.

No one knew exactly when that was. Their mother had been a prostitute and by the time boys were seven, she'd died of a drug overdose. None had a clue as to who was their father? Most likely he was a sailor in port for a few days and long gone. When the assigned Social Worker who had been handling their case showed up in the basement apartment that was their home address, she found them filthy and unwashed. Their mother's corpse was hidden beneath a blanket on the only bed in their rat-infest hovel. The woman called the police who in turn notified the coroner. Two days later Alice Bonello was buried in the city's potters field and the boys taken to the Ridgeway Orphanage for Boys in Castle Harbor, a small village community a few miles north of Cape Noire.

The orphanage wasn't much better than a prison for the young boys it sheltered and life there was hard. The Director was a cruel bastard who barely managed to keep his charges fed and clothed. Every winter at least three or four boys would die of pneumonia for lack of proper heating and nutrition. The state refused to inspect the facility too closely because that would have meant having to shut it down and that would have left them with the same damn problem. What to do with the unwanted kids?

But Jack and Tommy were never alone. They had each other and by then had realized it was a unique advantage they could not only exploit in their daily battle to survive, but also rely on no matter how bleak their situations. Once that was understood, the brothers escaped the orphanage two years later. They ran off one early summer morning, jumping in the back of a vegetable truck on its way to the city.

Once back in Cape Noire, Jack and Tommy became street urchins doing whatever it took for them to get by. They found shelter in abandoned buildings and warehouses and stole whatever else they required from food to clothing. In four years time they learned every back street and alley in Cape Noire and how to use them to escape both the police and rival youth gangs. In the city's underbelly of petty crime and larceny, the Bone Brothers became celebrities in their own fashion.

It became more and more of a problem because folks recognized them immediately. It was impossible to hide the fact they were the mirror image of each other. By the time they reached Delmont's Bakery, Jack had pulled a crumbled, filthy newsboy cap from his back pocket and put it on. He tugged the front down over his forehead, gave Tommy a nod and they walked into the small, crowded shop.

It was mid-morning and Old Man Delmont was behind the long counter serving customers, all crowded together. His oldest daughter, Clarice was working alongside him and both were busy grabbing donuts off the rows of shelves behind them and stuffing them into small brown paper bags. Once an order was filled, Delmont or Clarice would ring it up at the cash register located at the right end of the counter behind which was the swinging door to the kitchen.

As always, the smell of the place was heavenly and Jack wormed his way among several adults, keeping his head down.

"Hey, stop shoving?" an irate middle aged woman snapped as he came up next to her. Old Man Delmont turned to her, and Jack quickly made sure she was blocking the man's view. He and Tommy had hit the bakery quite a view times and the bushy haired Delmont knew them all too well.

In fact he kept a baseball bat under the counter that he swore he'd one day use to knock their blocks off.

"Here's your order, Mrs. Wren," he said, handing her the bag and moving to the register while wiping his hands on his apron. "That will be three dollars."

The woman pushed past others to join him which then opened the space for Jack. Clarice turned at that moment and asked, "Who's next?"

"I'll have four honey dip donuts," Jack said, dropping the timber of his voice to disguise it.

Without thinking twice, the tall, plump girl spun around, grabbed another paper sack and quickly filled it with four of the glazed round delights.

"Here you go," she smiled handing it to Jack.

He grabbed the bag, lifted his head and winked. "Thanks, doll face," before turning for the door.

"PA! It's one of the Bonellos!"

Hearing that, Jack shoved two men out of his way and reached the exit. He pulled open the door and turned right.

"Come back here you little bastard!" Old Man Delmont yelled loudly, as he came charging out of his bakery, a thick Louisville slugger held up in his right hand. "I'm gonna brain you good, you piece of shi—"

Just then, Tommy Bonello, who had been standing up against the wall, to Delmont's right, stuck out his right leg and the old man tripped over it, landing face first onto the cement sidewalk. Tommy laughed, stepped on the baker's back, pushing down hard as he did so and took off after Jack, laughing all the while.

Clarice Delmont came out of the store, saw her father and dropped to her knees beside him. "Pa! Are you all right?"

Old Man Delmont lifted his face, blood seeping from his nose, his chin all scratched up. "Do I look all right to you?" He swore under his breath before starting to get to his feet. Clarice helped him back into the shop, the baseball bat forgotten on the curb.

Jack and Tommy turned into the first alley they came to and then, finding a clean spot between two trash filled dumpsters, sat down to enjoy their donuts. Both were chuckling, recalling the look of surprise on Old

Man Delmont's face when he'd tripped over Tommy's leg.

"Splat," Jack laughed, slapping his knee as he chewed on his first bite of the gooey honey-covered pastry. "Just like in them cartoons at the movies."

Tommy merely nodded, as he munched away on a donut.

Both of them were oblivious to the figure rushing towards them from the street.

"Gotcha now, you street rats!" Just like that, Officer Milo Murphy was standing over them, his hardwood Billy club raised over his head.

The club came down and caught Jack on the shoulder with a loud whack. He cried out and fell onto his right side, the half eaten donut squashed in his fist.

Instinctively Tommy Bonello kicked out with his right leg. It hit Murphy in the left shin and he grimaced, quickly falling back a step. "Aw, you want a little of this too, do ya?" Again he held up his stick. "Gonna teach you bastards good, I am."

Tommy brought up his arms and let them absorb the hard blow. Pain lanced through his left arm and he thought it might be broken.

Hearing his brother yell out, Jack frantically looked around the garbage-strewn ground for something to use as a weapon. He spotted several old bricks. Tossing aside the bits of donuts still in his hand, he grabbed one of them. He then twisted his body around in time to see the copper striking at Tommy a second time. Lifting himself off the pavement with his left hand, Jack brought the brick around and hit their attacker across the left side of his face.

Officer Murphy stumbled back, his face smarting beneath a bruised cheekbone.

"Aghh—" he clutched at the spot only to increase the pain radiating there.

Seeing the distraction, Tommy rolled over and purposely plowed into the officer's legs. Murphy fell back, swinging out wildly with his Billy club. His sight was blurred by the sharp pain throbbing at the left side of his face. He never saw Jack Bonello jump up until it was too late.

Jack hit Murphy in the face, breaking his nose and knocking him senseless. The sadistic copper toppled over like a fallen tree. His uniform cap fell off his head.

"Is he dead?" Tommy asked getting to his feet warily. His left arm was hurting badly.

"Not yet," Jack replied, looking at the brick still in his hand. He then used it again; this time crushing the top of Murphy's head. The sound of the skull cracking was brutally loud. The cop's body shuddered and then was still forever.

Jack tossed the break away.

"Holy crap!" his brother exclaimed. "Guess that flatfoot won't be bothering us again. Ha."

Jack smiled and then reached across the dead man's body to unbutton the holster strapped to the right hip.

"Whatcha doing, Jack?"

"Getting *this*," Jack held up the .38 Police Special revolver, a gleam in his eyes. "He won't be needing this anymore."

"Yeah. Right. Let's check his pockets and see if he's got any extra bullets for it."

After a few minutes the brothers had found two dozen rounds in a small leather pouch, a pocket knife, handkerchief and a wallet containing forty-three dollars. Counting the bills, Jack looked at Tommy and slapped him on the arm. "Come, let's go get us a real breakfast. Courtesy of Officer Murphy." He lifted the back of his sweater and slipped the gun under his belt then made sure it was hidden from view as they exited the alley laughing.

Behind them, a half dozen rats stuck their noses out of from the behind the dumpsters. Smelling death, they began to emerge and investigate.

CHAPTER (3)

As the afternoon clouds dissipated over Forest Hill Cemetery, Harry Beest looked around at what was easily the largest funeral he had ever attended in his life. Being a career criminal, Beest had been to many such farewell gatherings. Some, in fact, he'd perpetrated. These black thoughts floated through his mind as he stood in the second row of primary mourners directly behind his employer, Mr. Topper Wyld; the acknowledged Crime Boss of Cape Noire.

Inside the rich mahogany casket, resting in folds of thick pink velvet, were the remains of Mrs. Eleanor Wyld, age thirty-six, recently deceased due to breast cancer. For Mrs. Wyld, the cares and worries of this world were gone. Not so for her husband, who stood stoically before the freshly dug grave dressed in a fine tan overcoat with a fur-lined collar and a fancy brown homburg on his head, soft kid gloves covering his bony hands. Wyld was fifty, with sharp, vulture-like facial features that included a pointed chin, hooked nose and small, piercing black eyes; all enhanced by a pale pink complexion. He spent very little time outside his five acre mansion with its eight-foot, guarded stone wall surrounding it.

Topper Wyld had only loved a few people in his life. Eleanor had been one of these. The other was his precocious twelve-year-old daughter, Alexis, who now stood between him and the brunette young lady to her left who was her nanny. Wyld had hired Yvette Minault after his wife had fallen sick, along with a private nurse. The cancer had quickly robbed Eleanor of her vitality and forced her to be bedridden and unable to care for a frightened little girl. Thus Miss Minault's arrival at the recommendation of their family doctor had proven most beneficial. She was an intelligent, congenial young woman who had easily wormed her way into the family's good graces. She had quickly established a strong bond with Alexis, who badly needed more emotional support than her father could ever provide. There was no doubt that Topper Wyld adored his daughter, but he had always been a cruel, hard man and simply did not possess the means to effectively communicating that affection.

His idea of loving his lovely, pre-teen heir was to see that she was taken care of with all the comforts he could provide for her. Occasionally he might manage a hug or a kiss on the cheek. Never the lips. Alexis would simply have to do with that. It was all he could offer. Whereas the nanny was overly affectionate, friendly, and—most of all—understanding. In her arms, Alexis had cried long and hard on the night her mother died. Thus Yvette Minault would always have a special place in the girl's heart.

It didn't hurt that she was also a looker, Harry Beest reflected letting his eyes travel down the nanny's backside. From where he stood the view was more than nice. She was of average height, with a shape men ogled. Long, gorgeous legs, a tight ass, slim waist and a most generous, healthy bust that couldn't be hidden behind her tight silk blouses. At the funeral, she'd dressed appropriately in black; high heels, seamed stockings, a pencil skirt and short jacket. A see-through black veil covered her long jet-black tresses that touched her shoulders.

Her face was angelic, with a dimpled chin, heart-shape red lips, a straight nose, and two bright azure-blue eyes that seemed to be on fire.

Yeah, a real knock-out, Beest imagined what she would look like in her birthday suit. It was something he'd been looking forward to ever since Ms. Minault had joined the household. Now with Mrs. Wyld gone, it was a good bet the nanny would be around for a while longer. That suited Beest just fine.

Beest considered himself a lady's man as his past conquests would attest to. From an early age, his rugged good looks and dark wavy hair had worked to his benefit in charming women of all ages. Even as a teen, he'd catch neighborhood girls eyeing him whenever he and his pals marched along the dirty, crowded, low-rent tenement zones that were their playgrounds. What had initially surprised him was that their mothers also seemed to smile a little more when he was around them. Their cheeks would turn a little redder and some would go as far as to playfully pat his side when he was near. That older, married women would flirt with him was a revelation he quickly learned to appreciate. It proved most helpful when he was chasing their nubile teenage daughters.

Hey, if he couldn't win over the girl, he reasoned, why not give the old lady a try?

His thought-train instantly brought him back to Jerry Guicci's wanton old lady, Marla. He was fifteen the summer afternoon he stopped by their apartment on Conklin only to learn that Jerry had already gone out with a bunch of other guys.

Standing in the open door, a cigarette dangling from her mouth, Marla had delivered the news with a bored look on her face. At thirty-two she still had a body men took notice of. She was wearing a loose dress, tied with a belt about her waist. Her blouse was unbuttoned and Harry could see she wasn't wearing a bra. Her round tits were all but spilling out. When he didn't move from the spot, Marla realized exactly what it was the boy was looking at, and then a strange smile widened her lips.

Before he knew what was happening, she reached out, took hold of his tee-shirt and pulled him into the apartment, slamming the door shut behind him.

That afternoon, in the bed she shared with her mechanic husband, Marla Guicci educated Harry Beest on the myriad ways of satisfying a woman. It was an education he never forgot, and though there would be many, many other women in his life, the memory of that afternoon would remain with him forever. Bottom line, Marla had taught him that men weren't the only ones who liked to screw. Women could be just as sexually hungry; maybe even more so.

A cool breeze through the trees around them, snapped Beest out of his delicious reverie. His attention once again reverted to the large assembly gathered on the freshly-mowed grass. He had no problems recognizing the other mob chiefs and their men; a few had even brought along their broads or wives, whatever the case may be. Mixed among these lowlifes were a few high-ranking political figures including Cape Noire's own

Deputy Mayor Steve Ungersham and next to him Police Commissioner Clark Whitmore.

Talk about balls, Beest thought. *Goes to show just how powerful the boss is when the muckety-muck big shots show up at his wife's send off.*

Beest knew all Topper Wyld had to do was snap his fingers and these men jumped. The boss owned Cape Noire and everyone and his uncle knew it.

That included the dozen or so newspaper and radio standing across the field by the road where at least seven of Commissioner Whitmore's boys-in-blue were making sure the uninvited were kept far away from the somber ceremony.

"Dust to dust, ashes to ashes," Protestant Rev. Hiram Linquist intoned, holding his worn prayer book in his hands. He was a small man with gray hair and flat nose. "Secure in our faith looking for the general Resurrection in the last day. Raised up for all eternity through the grace of Our Lord, Jesus Christ. Amen."

As several others echoed his amen, Rev. Linquist reached down and took a handful of dirt from the mound behind him. He then tossed it atop the casket and nodded to Wyld. Silently, the widower copied the minister's gesture and added his handful of dirt. One by one, others in the party followed suit. Wyld took Alexis's hand and started walking away.

Disliking the morbid gesture of finality symbolized by the dirt throwing, Harry Beest simply turned and followed after the others making sure to stay close to Wyld. Even if he doubted any of the other participants stupid enough to try anything at such a solemn affair, his job was to protect and serve his master. He could only do that if he was Topper Wyld's constant shadow. Thus he increased his pace to ascertain he was never more than a few feet away from the crime boss.

Wyld led the procession up to where a line of automobiles were parked. His silver Cadillac was at the head and the driver, a rat-faced hood named Reed Vengel, was leaning against the grill smoking a cigarette.

"Topper," a voice spoke out softly from behind the entourage.

Beest looked to his left to see Big Swede Jorgenson moving through the crowd, followed by two of his own gunsels. Jorgenson was another powerful mob figure, though considered by most as second to Wyld; a fact he didn't seem to mind. For the time being, he seemed to be okay with his place in the hierarchy. Or so Harry Beest had been led to believe by word on the streets.

Wyld stopped at the curb and waited for Big Swede to reach him.

"Swede," he acknowledged coolly. "Thank you for coming."

"I'm truly sorry for your loss," the tall, fair skinned gangster said. "Please accept my condolences." He extended his hand and Wyld took it without hesitating.

"That's kind of you. Thank you."

"In matters of the heart, we are all the same, eh?" Jorgenson shrugged. "Things like family and loved ones are what are truly important in this world."

"Wise words. Again, thank you."

Both men smiled at each other before Swede signaled his men and they strolled off toward their own ride.

Meanwhile, Vengel had tossed away his butt end and hurried to the Caddy's back door which he now held open. Wyld, Alexis and Miss Minault all climbed into the back. Harry Beest went around the front end and took the front passenger seat as Vengel started the engine, gave it some gas and pointed the car down the small dirt lane towards the cemetery's exit.

CHAPTER (4)

By the time word got to the 8th Precinct that one of their own had been discovered dead in a dirty Thatcher St. alley, the rats had done a very nasty job on the late Officer Murphy's face. Half a dozen good size chunks of skin had been gnawed off including the tip of his now cold nose.

"Yeah, that's Murphy all right," Lt. Detective Clement Serat confirmed while lighting the cigarette in his mouth. He flicked out the small match flame and then took a long drag of nicotine. He preferred smoking Lucky Strikes without those new filter tips that were the latest thing among cigarette manufacturers. Obviously intended to attract the female half of the population, he figured. He pulled the cigarette from his thin lips and spat out a tiny piece of tobacco.

Serat was in his late fifties, average height with a rapidly growing paunch; the guys in the squad room teased him about it constantly. Hey, it wasn't his fault his old lady was such a good cook. He had a beefy face, distinguished by a thick gray mustache that would have made a walrus proud, with matching eyebrows. He wore a dark green suit with a corresponding high-crown fedora that had seen lots of better days.

By now he'd normally have had his worn notebook in his pudgy hands and been writing down his observations of the crime scene. But today had proved to be his lucky day. He had been assigned Cape Noire's newly minted rookie bull: Detective First Grade Daniel Rains. Hence, upon arriving at the location in their unmarked sedan, Serat had immediately ordered Rains to do the honors.

"Write down everything you see and hear. Got that, Rains?"

"Yes, sir. Will do."

"And don't *sir*, me," the senior bull corrected. "We're partners. Serat will do just fine."

"Yes, si…I mean, okay."

Typical of all new dicks, Rains was having a hard time containing his own anxieties; this being his first call since getting his gold shield. In his time Serat had seen lots of them come and go. Whether the tall, lanky Rains would be one of the tough ones who made it had yet to be determined. Cape Noire ate up cops with weak stomachs. Like all jungles, it was a place where the strong survived and the weak did not regardless of which side of the legal fence they inhabited.

The detectives had been greeted by two uniform officers: Paul Malloy and Terrence Duseault. Like the detectives, both were assigned to this part of the city and familiar with its streets and twisted labyrinth of alleyways. They'd also known the dead man.

"Was bound to happen sooner or later," Officer Duseault stated matter-of-factly, standing over the corpse. "Murphy was an asshole who liked to push people around."

Serat exhaled a cloud of smoke. "You saying he wasn't loved and admired by the fine people of the neighborhood?"

"More like they put up with him," Officer Malloy chimed in. He was half African and half Asian; his face displaying exotic features one didn't usually see in these parts.

Serat squatted down and pointed to the head. "Considering someone bashed in his skull, it's fairly obvious he pissed off the wrong people this time around."

"Right," Duseault agreed and he also pointed. "They lifted his sidearm."

At that, Detective Serat's head looked to the empty holster. "Aw, shit!" He stood up and shook his head. "That's just great. Not only is the Chief going to have a conniption fit, but that means our report is going to require goddamn twice as much paperwork."

He looked to his new partner wondering if the kid had anything to add.

"Well, it's standard procedure, right?" Rains offered cautiously.

"Yeah, kid, it freakin' is."

They all heard an automobile approaching and watched in momentary silence as the City Coroner's black ambulance rolled up. Serat recognized the coroner, Dr. Art Sippo, as he exited the vehicle, along with several attendants carrying a canvas stretcher.

Sippo, a little guy with round glasses, went straight to the remains, nodding to Serat as he did so.

"Serat."

"Doc."

"Hmm, someone really didn't like this guy," Sippo said wryly.

"We were just discussing that very topic."

On his knees, examining the large bloody dent in Murphy's head, Dr. Sippo glanced around. Seeing a discarded brick only a few feet away, he stood up and retrieved it. He turned it over in his hands and found strands of hair coagulated within a dried, red, sticky glob of blood.

"Looks like the cause of death," Sippo observed dryly. "Though I doubt we'll get any prints off its surface."

The two men with the stretcher approached and Sippo told them to go ahead and collect the body. Meanwhile Serat asked the two blues who it was that had called in the discovery.

"Some wino walking by," Malloy replied. "Called the precinct from a nearby drugstore about thirty minutes ago."

"I don't suppose he agreed to come in and give a statement?"

"In this neighborhood? Are you kidding?"

Serat shrugged. There was no getting around what came next. It was time to hit the pavement. "All right, let's do it by the numbers." He pointed to Malloy. "You and I will canvas the south side of the street. Rains, you and Duseault take the north. I know it's a long shot, but just maybe today we'll get lucky and somebody will remember seeing something."

As the late Officer Murphy was loaded into the back of the ambulance, his four colleagues began their investigation.

For Dan Rains, who had come up through the ranks at the 10th Precinct—which was closer to downtown—the Thatcher street district was new to him. He wisely suggested to Officer Duseault that he be the one to question store owners and any other people loitering within the block.

Their first few meetings with shop clerks proved fruitless until they walked into Delmont's Bakery. The minute Officer Duseault asked the baker if he or his daughter had seen anything in regards to Officer Murphy that day, Old Man Delmont all but jumped over the counter at them.

"I saw him!" he said, waving his hands over his head. "It was after those two brats came in here and stole some of my donuts."

"When was this?" Rains pulled out his notebook and pencil.

"Around ten, this morning," Delmont looked to Clarice. "Eh, right?"

"Yeah, Pa. Just after ten."

"So what exactly happened, Mr. Delmont?"

"Those sons of Satan. That's what happened. They come marching in here and while we was busy with our customers, one of them grabbed a bag of donuts and ran out the door. I went after him, only to have the other one waiting outside. The little bastard tripped me so they could get away."

Rains was scribbling fast. "What happened next?"

"That's when Murphy came walking by, like he does every day. He saw Clarice helping me up and asked what had happened. I told him and then he ran off after them."

Rains stopped writing and looked up. "Them. Do you know who they were?"

Delmont gave Rains a queer look. "You must be new here, fella. Everyone on the streets around here knows the Bone Brothers."

"Who?"

"The twins, Jack and Tommy Bonello. We call them the Bone Brothers."

Before Detective Rains could ask anything else, Officer Duseault tilted his cap back and said, "Aw, shit!"

Butch Hammer spent his first two days in Cape Noire looking for work. Luck wasn't with him despite his smattering of skills. The few auto garages he checked out simply weren't hiring and that was the same response he was given at the two gyms he visited with the help of the telephone book yellow pages.

On the third day, he decided to go down to the docks and see if he might be able sign up with a local stevedore's union. It was just after noon when he stepped off the bus at a busy street corner in front of a place called The Gridiron Saloon. Taped to the glass window was a crude cardboard sign reading "Help Wanted."

He stood there for a few seconds after the bus pulled away and looked down the long row of piers, docks and giant seagoing tankers. The taste of brine was in the cool air. The road was congested with lots of trucks moving to and fro between the anchored vessels, under giant cranes, loading cargo and disappearing into the several side streets jam packed with giant warehouses.

Hammer had worked on the docks back in Jersey. It was tough, dirty work and really didn't pay much. So he looked at the cardboard sign and shrugged.

What the hell?

He stepped into the saloon and was immediately assaulted by the sounds and smells of the crowded tavern. The main room was a long rectangular area, with an enclosed telephone booth to his immediate left, then there were cafe seating booths going all the way to the back wall. The narrow center aisle was crammed with patrons of every race and hue. He wasn't at all surprised to see Asian sailors, mingling with Americans. Considering the city was located on the shores of the Mighty Pacific, it was only logical that much of their commerce was done with countries like China and Japan and all the other Pacific Rim cultures. He had also discovered a thriving Chinese neighborhood during his initial exploration of the city.

At the back of the saloon, through the thick haze of cigarette and cigar smoke, he could make out a metal sign which extended from the wall labeled PRIVY, and beyond that another door he assumed exited to a back alley.

To the right was the bar itself; a long running counter set up with at least twenty-padded stools in front of it. Behind the bar the wall split in the middle with an open doorway. Long steel shelves were filled with liquor bottles of every known variety, while rising up behind the polished, rich mahogany surface were colorful, hand-carved handles that Hammer knew were affixed to beer barrel spigots.

The noise itself was deafening with people at the booths jawing away loudly competing to be heard over the voices of those at the bar. Through the tight little aisle, a frazzled looking redheaded female, with an apron around her middle, was pushing against the human tide while holding up a tray with three mugs of beer on it. Somehow she miraculously reached her destination, set down the tray to the delight of three happy drinkers. She collected their money and then started her battle back to the bar.

Taking this all in, Hammer spotted a small Chinaman vacating a stool and immediately shoved his way to it. Sitting down, he dropped his travel

"WHAT THE HELL?"

kit on the copper foot pedestal that ran the length of the bar six inches off the floor.

"So, what'll you have, pally?" a gruff voice assaulted him.

Its owner was a squat, square-shaped woman with curly gray hair, a broken nose and a cigar in her mouth. She wore a heavy plaid man's shirt, the sleeves rolled up past the elbows of her thick arms. The left one had the tattoo of a tiger on it. All of this would have been startling enough without the huge brown eyes that animated her entire being. They reminded Hammer of the fancy marbles he played with as a child.

"Well, aside from a beer…"

"Speak up," she interrupted leaning over the bar. "So's I can hear you."

Hammer brought his head closer and raised his voice. "I wanted to talk to you about that job you've got up for grabs."

"Well, why da hell didn't you say so?" the woman bellowed, slapping a hand down on the bar. "Get your ass off that stool and come around here."

"What?"

"The job," she all but shouted. "If you want it, get back here. You start right now. Or don't you think we need the help?" At that she smiled and he was shocked she actually had all her teeth, though they were a bit stained. *Cigars will do that*, Hammer thought as he grabbed his kit, dropped off his stool and pushed himself through the mass of bodies to get to the end of the long counter.

Once back there, the woman greeted him with another toothy smile.

"I'm Molly McCoy, follow me." She then disappeared into the open space between the wall shelves. Hammer hurried behind her and within two steps found himself standing in the middle of a tiny kitchen complete with counters to either side of the doorway, a stove, and a deep steel sink to the right with a huge ice box to the left. To the right of the ice box was another door.

"That goes to the cellar and our supplies," Molly McCoy waving at door with her cigar. Then she turned and looked at Butch Hammer from the toe of his boots to the top of his knit cap.

"What's yer name, pally?"

"Hammer. Folks call me Butch."

"Can you make a decent sandwich, Butch?" She indicated the nearest counter where loaves of bread, condiments and sharp knives were waiting. Among with these were several sausage rolls of salami, pepperoni and baloney in various lengths.

"Yeah, I can make a sandwich," he shrugged.

"Good. In the upper cabinets you'll find various bread loafs from rye to pumpernickel. Only use those if asked for them specifically. Otherwise use white bread. And don't cut the meat too skinny or the boys won't like it. When you make 'em a sandwich, make it a big ole chunk. Then slather on the mustard and add a pickle from that jar over there.

"More of those in the ice box, along with rest of the sausage rolls. You got all that?"

Hammer began to take off his jacket. "I think so. You ever do hot food?"

As McCoy reached under the sink to grab him a clean apron, she nodded to the stove in the corner by the sink. "Only in the winter, when we do soup and chowder. Keep the guys warm and toasty. Winters on those docks are brutal."

Hammer was looking to where he could toss his hat and jacket when the waitress with the red locks joined them.

"Ma, I need two baloney sandwiches and one pepperoni," she declared tossing an oval shaped tray on the counter. She saw Hammer and arched an eyebrow. He saw it was the same orange rust color as her hair. Up close, she was actually pretty.

"Butch, this here is my daughter, Peggy. Peggy, this is Butch Hammer, our new employee."

"Nice to meetcha," she smiled, blowing a strand of lose hair off her face. "Hustle it up with those sandwiches, will ya."

"Sure thing," he said, but she was already gone. He looked at her mother puzzled.

"She's a cyclone, that one," Molly McCoy grinned blowing out a pull of smoke. "She handles the booths all by herself. Never saw anyone move so fast on her feet. When you ain't making food back here, you'll be up front with me behind the bar.

"That okay with you?"

"Sure thing," he tied the apron about his middle. "I've a worked in a few bars back east in my time."

"That where you're from, the East?"

"Yeah, got in two days ago." He grabbed a knife and the big pepperoni sausage and set it on the long chopping block atop the counter. Deftly he sliced off a thick slab.

"Where you staying?"

"Got a room at a boarding house downtown."

McCoy watched Hammer cut a few more chunks of meat and then he started slapping yellow mustard on slices of bread. She liked what she was seeing. He was efficient and looking at his hands, she could see rough calluses. This guy wasn't afraid of hard work.

"Pay is thirty-five dollars a week," she informed him. "Also got two apartments upstairs. Peggy and I live in one of them. You can have the other no charge, if you take the job. It's not the Taj Mahal, but it's clean and got its own bath and running water."

Butch Hammer stopped assembling the sandwiches and after a silent pause, wiped his hands on the blue checkered apron around his waist and extended his right hand.

"I'll take it, Mrs. McCoy and thanks."

"You lose that Missus stuff, I'm just Ma to everyone." She grabbed his hand and squeezed it tight. "Got that."

For the first time in months, Butch Hammer smiled happily. "Got it!"

CHAPTER (5)

It was almost midnight when Harry Beest brought the expensive silver Cadillac to a stop in front of the dilapidated brownstone located at 909 Old Town Way. It was an ominous looking affair at the end of a lonely street. The less than savory neighborhood was one of many neighborhoods inhabited by the city's poor and wretched souls.

"You got to be kidding me," he mouthed, shutting off the engine.

In the back seat, Topper Wyld looked up at the grim three story structure and merely shrugged. "I was told the professor was an odd duck. Brilliant, but strange. Ergo setting this meeting at this unusual hour."

Beest felt uneasy. The street itself was sparse with only a few other houses on the block, each situated far apart from the others. The streetlamps were few and offered very little in the way of illumination. Though there were lights visible on the first floor of the house.

"It's like something out of a horror movie."

"You're not afraid of monsters, are you, Harry?"

"Not afraid of anything I can see," the hitman replied. "It's what I can't see that bothers me."

"Well, let's not keep the good doctor waiting, shall we."

That was Beest's cue to get out of the car, open the back door and await his employer's exit. Topper Wyld stepped onto the sidewalk, as Beest shut the back door gently. Then the big man unconsciously tapped his sports jacket breast to feel the .45 automatic seated snuggly in its leather holster.

Even this little assurance was a comfort.

The two of them walked up the seven cement steps to the front entrance and Wyld stood off to the side of the massive door as Beest punched the doorbell. The action produced several ringing chimes within the house and they waited patiently for a response. It arrived in minutes and the door was pulled back by a veritable giant in human guise.

Beest's neck arched as he looked up at the man before him; clearly seven feet tall if an inch with a face that looked liked it had been battered in a cement mixer. The forehead protruded over sunken eye sockets, and the man's jaw was extended in surrounding two fat lips. The grim looking fellow wore a somber gray uniform, with brown shoes the size of watermelons.

"Yes," he growled, his voice as deep a bottomless cellar.

"Topper Wyld to see Professor Bugosi."

The ugly manservant stepped back allowing them to enter. "He is waiting for you in the office. Follow me."

Beest let his boss take the lead and closed the door behind them as the trio then marched down a dark, dank hallway that was devoid of any furnishings. Only two small lights were set in the high ceiling. He was surprised there were no carpets on the dark hardwood floors which looked as if they had not been cleaned since the coming of Columbus.

Harry Beest had the itch to sneeze and rubbed his index finger against his nostrils to dispel it. Wouldn't be good manners to let out a honker behind the boss. At the end of the hall was an elevator in the right corner. Across from this was an open door from which light spilled. This was the large den into which the big man led them.

It was Spartan with two massive desks set at both ends of the room. Each was fronted by two red leather chairs. Tall standing lamps provided garish light that cast eerily-shaped shadows on the walls. As the trio entered the room, Professor Lazlo Bugosi rose from behind the desk to their right and came over to greet them.

He was of average height, with jet black hair worn short and smeared with hair promenade so that it looked like a cap set atop his skull. Matching arched eyebrows flared over two small, piercing eyes and his white complexion attested to a life lived primarily indoors. He wore a somber black suit, with a white shirt and gray tie.

Offering his hand to Topper Wyld, he smiled. "Welcome to my humble abode, Mr. Wyld."

"A pleasure to meet you, Professor Bugosi," Wyld replied, shaking the hand once. "Or would your prefer being called Doctor?"

The tiny eyes crinkled. "As both honorifics are appropriate, choose whichever suits you, sir."

"Then Professor it shall be."

Bugosi pointed to the leather chairs. "Please be seated, gentlemen."

Wyld unbuttoned his topcoat and removed his hat, looking back at the chair. Seeing this, Bugosi looked to his assistant and snapped his fingers. "Waldo, see to Mr. Wyld's coat and hat."

"Yes, Professor," the man nodded and quickly obeyed.

"Thank you," Wyld nodded, handing Waldo his expensive outer garments. Then he turned and indicated Beest. "This is my associate, Harry Beest."

Bugosi eyed Beest politely and recognized him for what he was; a devoted and dangerous bodyguard. "Would you gentlemen care for a drink?"

"I'm fine," Wyld answered as he sat down.

"I could go for a beer," Beest admitted.

Bugosi again directed his words to his aide. "Waldo, be so kind as to get a beer from the kitchen icebox for our guest."

At that the lumbering figure exited the den and Bugosi returned to his straight back padded chair behind his desk.

They could hear the servant's heavy footsteps gradually fading away in the hall.

"Waldo suffers from a condition known as Acromegaly which distorts the features of the face. He's been cruelly ostracized by others most of his adult life. My employment and support is the only kindness he has ever known. I hope his radical disfigurement did frighten you?"

"I'll confess, it was a surprise, initially," Wyld admitted, comfortably resting one leg over the other. "But I've seen more than my share of such oddities in my life, Professor. This is, after all, Cape Noire."

"It most certainly is a unique and interesting city," Bugosi concurred. He brought his hands up together atop his desk and interlaced his fingers. "I want to thank you for coming, Mr. Wyld and at such a late hour. You must wonder as to my arranging our meeting at long last."

"I am, Professor. After receiving your invitation, I had my people do a background search beyond the known details. You're not the average citizen, after all."

At that Bugosi laughed. It was a melodious sound much like that of a playful child. "Ah, yes, what is it the papers have labeled me? 'The Mad

Scientist of Cape Noire.' How whimsical, is it not?"

"Well, you're background is rather checkered, Professor," Wyld continued. "Originally from Hungry, you studied at several prestigious universities throughout Europe, and then ended up working for the Germans during the war. There are some who say you helped them invent Mustard Gas.

"Then after the war, you fled the continent ahead of several international warrants for your arrest and eventually ended up here three years ago."

Bugosi's face remained stoic, not giving away anything.

Guy's got a natural poker face, Harry Beest thought.

"The charges against me were never proven," the scientist said. "And attempts to have me arrested and deported were all prevented by your country's State Department. Much to my gratitude." Bugosi opened his hand and gestured the room about them. "And now I am free to go about my research without hindrance."

At that moment Waldo returned holding a small steel tray on which was a cold bottle of beer. He went to Beest and lowered the tray before him.

"Thanks," Beest held up the bottle in a salute and then took a long drink emptying half its contents with one long swallow. He wiped his lips with the back of his free hand and smiled. "Much appreciated, Professor."

"You are most welcome, Mr. Beest." Bugosi's plastered-on smile remained frozen in place. He then gave Waldo new commands. "Waldo, go to the lab and prepare my materials for the demonstration."

"At once, Master." Waldo made a second exit.

Without turning his head, Wyld addressed his host. "Demonstration?"

"Ah, yes. The reason why I requested this meeting," Bugosi explained. "Mr. Wyld, are you familiar with the stories of British writer, Robert Louis Stevenson?"

"I'm not much of a reader, Professor. If they didn't teach it in at PS 85 where I went to school, then it doesn't concern me. Arithmetic was more by forte, if you will. The foundations of my, shall we say, fondness for business."

"But of course," Bugosi conceded. "My intent was to reference one particular novel by the esteemed Mr. Stevenson; 'The Strange Case of Dr. Jekyll and Mr. Hyde.' It is about a doctor, not unlike myself, obsessed with learning the mysteries of the human psyche. That is, what makes some men good and others bad.

"His Doctor Jekyll believes there exist in all of us a duality and he desires to separate the two halves. To eliminate the evil in himself."

"You'll excuse me, Professor, but that in itself sounds mad," Topper Wyld interrupted. "Men are what their decisions make them. A priest will never be a killer nor will a killer become a saint."

Bugosi's sardonic smile remained fixed. He sighed. "But what if one could enhance one's character traits?"

"Meaning exactly what?"

"What if I could bring out the feral beast in a living creature and make it ten times stronger than its true nature dictated? Would that in fact be an application worthy of note?"

Wyld was not a stupid man. Yet the scientist's words seemed beyond his understanding and that frustrated him.

"Look, Bugosi, can you cut to the chase. Why am I here and what the hell is it you are talking about?"

"Aha, at last." Bugosi clapped his hands happily and rose from his chair. "Please, Mr. Wyld, come with me and I will show you exactly why I have brought you here. And answer all your questions at the same time so that all will be made perfectly clear."

The mob boss looked at the scientist, shrugged and stood up. Harry Beest did the same and together they let their host usher them out of the den. Bugosi led them down the corridor to the elevator they'd seen earlier. He tapped a button and the steel door slid open.

"Gentlemen, if you will," he smiled indicating the empty interior. Wyld and Beest stepped in. Then Bugosi entered and punched the top button to the left of the door. The door slid shut; the elevator shook slightly and then began to rise.

"My laboratory is on the second floor," he told them. The ride lasted less than a minute and then the door opened once again. The three walked into a brightly lit cavernous room with dozens of harsh halogen lights suspended from the ceiling.

Harry Beest had never seen a laboratory and the layout before him was both fascinating and strange. Along both walls were long steel tables, on which were various electrically powered machines. Situated among these were test tubes, Bunsen burners and other gadgets whose function were a mystery. The hum of static electricity permeated the air and Beest felt the hairs on the back of his neck react.

Then as they moved to the center of the long room, he saw Waldo down on one knee by the far wall beside a dog. The animal was a typical mongrel like hundreds of others seen on the streets every day. It stood a little over two feet in height, with yellow-brown fur, a short snout and floppy ears.

A leather collar was wrapped around its neck attached to a steel chain of several feet bolted into the wall. Waldo was affectionately rubbing the dog's back as it kept reaching up to lick his face.

"The animal Waldo is with was picked up at the city pound several weeks ago," Professor Bugosi began. "At the time it was in fairly good health and since bringing it here, Waldo as has made sure to keep it well fed and looked after."

"Isn't that so, Waldo?"

The big man looked up. "Yes, Professor. He's a good dog."

Without another word the scientist walked over to the nearest table on which were several test tubes, petri dishes and syringes. He picked one of the syringes, placed the tip of the needle into a small glass filled with a greenish liquid and then pulled out the plunger, causing the stuff to fill the clear container. This task completed, Bugosi went over to Waldo and told him to hold the canine firmly. He bent down and smoothly inserted the needle into the dog's flank. It gave a startled yip, but Waldo held it comfortably. After removing the needle, Bugosi rejoined his two guests still a good twenty feet away.

"As you can see, Mr. Wyld, the animal is a docile creature. It did not even growl or snap at me when being injected."

"So it's a good dog," Topper Wyld confirmed. "What now?"

"Now, we merely wait and watch."

Wyld turned to Beest and shrugged, as if to remind him of his comments back when they were in the car.

A minute passed and there seemed to be nothing happening to the animal. Then it slowly began to shake slightly. Its head started twisting back and forth. Instantly Waldo moved away from it, putting some distance between them as the animal's tremors grew more noticeable.

Suddenly its head lifted up and he barked. Both Topper Wyld and Harry Beest stepped back a step, startled.

The dog continued to bark louder and louder, its entire body convulsing as if in the grips of agonizing pain. Then it stopped. Spittle dropped from its mouth and a growl formed in its chest, which was now swelling.

"Is it getting bigger?" Wyld couldn't believe what he was seeing.

The dog's body was changing, almost doubling in size.

"Look at its eyes!" Harry Beest blurted out pointing. "They're red!"

The dog's growl was fierce and its eyes were indeed a deep red hue.

It lunged forward as far as the chain would allow it. Frustrated by the hold on its neck, the now altered animal continued to push against its bond, straining so violently the veins in its neck were visible.

There was a loud crack and the bolt in the wall ripped free. The freed savage dog charged towards the assembled men and sprang into the air, its fangs out ready to rip into them.

At which point, Waldo intercepted it in mid-air, his left arm holding the animal's body while his right immediately encircled its neck. Furious, the crazed mutt trying to turn its head but the man was too strong and fast.

Waldo snapped its neck, killing it instantly, ending its threat to Bugosi and the two gangsters.

"Holy shit!" gasped Harry Beest, standing beside Topper Wyld, his automatic in his hand ready to fire.

Professor Lazlo Bugosi turned to the Crime Boss of Cape Noire and asked, "So, Mr. Wyld, what do you think? Can you imagine what my potion could do to a man?"

"Are you saying it would have the same effects as what I just saw?" Wyld looked from the scientist to Waldo now holding the limp dead dog. His mind was racing with the possibilities."

"You could have an army of unstoppable soldiers," Bugosi suggested.

"But could they be controlled? From what I just saw, that was a wild beast."

"Agreed, the formula is not perfected yet. But in time, and with the proper funds, I hope to produce results that will still stimulate the subject's rage but at the same time make it possible to maintain its mental control during the transformation."

"You said you needed cash. How much are we talking here?"

"It is difficult to say, Mr. Wyld. I will need new equipment, chemicals... ah...*test subjects....*"

"I don't care," Wyld held up a hand. "Whatever you need, send me the bill. From now on I will bankroll your entire operations. I don't care what it costs."

"You are most generous."

"No, Bugosi. I'm just smart. Your only obligation is that whatever crazy stuff you cook up here is only for me exclusively. No one else. Agreed?" Wyld held out his hand.

"But of course," the Professor and the mobster shook cementing their new partnership of twisted evil.

Coming down the steps to the street, Topper Wyld was already contemplating what he could do with an army of monstrous men at his command.

"What do you think, Harry?" he asked his number one killer.

"Jeezus, Boss, that was some crazy shit. I don't know. You think this guy can do what he says?"

They started for Wyld's car.

"I'm betting on it, Harry. Because if he can, then in a few years' time, we are going to run this entire city. From every dock to gambling parlor, it will be ours. You, me and the boys wise enough to join up with us."

Beest pulled open the back door. "It sounds swell, Boss. But I still don't like that guy. He gives me the willies."

Topper Wyld settled himself in the backseat and smiled. "As long as Bugosi delivers, I don't give a damn about his personality. Now take us home, Harry. It's been a very long day."

Minutes later the Caddy rolled back into the street and drove off under a night sky dotted with stars and a white half moon.

CHAPTER (6)

Sandra Levine, better known as Sadie, sat at the counter in Lou's Diner finishing her breakfast of black coffee and bagel. It was all she could afford, as business had been dismal on the streets of Old Town the past few nights. A tall, heavy set black woman with shoulder length hair, Sadie had been a prostitute since the age of sixteen when her mother had kicked out her for trying to steal away her clients. Guess their tiny one room apartment in the Five Corners wasn't big enough for two whores. That was twelve years ago and somehow Sadie had managed to stay alive. Even if she hated every minute of it.

"Want a refill?" Gladys, the elderly white-haired waitress behind the counter asked holding up the steel pot. She'd seen Sadie's cup was almost empty.

"Sure, why not," Sadie held out the porcelain cup. "Thanks, Gladys."

"Rough night?" Gladys asked as she poured the steaming hot liquid into empty cup.

"When aren't they?"

"Sorry, kid."

"Not your fault, dearie." Sadie took a cautious sip of the hot java. "Cold nights keep the johns at home with their old ladies."

Having finished her bagel, Sadie dug into her small purse she'd put on the counter. Inside it were personal things—including a straight razor she'd learned how to use in defending herself against men who liked to hit women. Sadie was no fool and had long ago learned of all the various twisted habits her customers were addicted to. Most were laughable and she simply endured them as long as the john paid up.

But she wouldn't let any of them use her as a punching bag. That's where Sadie Levine drew the line. Over the years several had tried. One had even put her in the hospital with several broker ribs. Upon her release, she'd bought the razor. It was the last time a man ever laid a hand on her that wasn't open.

From the purse she pulled out a small box of cigarillos. She slipped one free and put it in her mouth while looking for a matchbook among the other loose items in the bag.

"Let me get that for you," a voice said from behind her.

Sadie swiveled around and beheld easily the fattest man she had ever seen. He stood approximately six feet in height with a round body that looked like a giant beach ball dressed in an expensive three piece. And it was expensive. The cut indicating it has been hand tailored. It was a pin-stripe charcoal gray, with a vest and natty dark blue tie. The owner's face was a smaller ball seated atop the bigger one with full cheeks, a button nose and two large blue eyes protected by one wire-framed glasses. He had thinning brown hair under a black bowler and a flower stick in his breast pocket button. His soft pudgy hands held a mahogany cane in the left while the right brandished a gold Zippo lighter.

He flicked the flame into life, his smile reminding Sadie of a winged cherub she'd seen pictures of. Only this angel would need a Zeppelin to lift him off the ground. She guessed his weight was well over three hundred pounds.

She leaned over and let the fire start her cigarillo. Inhaling, she moved back, removed the tobacco stick and blew out a puff of smoke.

"Thanks, Mister—?"

"Jacob Wiseman, Attorney at Law. At your service, Miss Levine."

"You know my name?"

"I know a great deal about you, madam. It is my client's wish that you accompany me on a little drive uptown."

"Your client?" she blew out another cloud. "And who might that be, Mr. Wiseman?"

"I represent Mr. Topper Wyld, Esquire," the fat man declared, his voice becoming instantly serious.

Few things affected Sadie enough to demonstrate emotional reactions but hearing the name of Topper Wyld was one of those. She sat up straight, her eyes showing recognition and respect for the man who owned it.

"Why's Topper Wyld interested in me?" What she was thinking was, *How the hell does the Crime Boss of Cape Noire even know I exist?* She didn't want to contemplate possible answers.

Jacob Wiseman merely smiled amusedly. "I assure you, Miss Levine, Mr. Wyld's interest is to your benefit and he wishes you only good fortune. In fact, you may consider this your lucky day."

Sadie couldn't possibly fathom what was going on. Who this Wiseman character was or why Topper Wyld would bother with a nobody prostitute like her? At the same time their conversation had quietly become the center of attention in the crowded diner and everyone, either at the counter or in the booths, was doing their best to look uninterested when in fact they were all ears.

"Please," Wiseman urged her politely. He pulled a five dollar bill out of his jacket pocket and dropped it on the counter by her purse. "Come with me and all will be explained. You have my word no harm will befall you while in my care."

Ah hell, she thought. *What do I gotta lose? Ain't like my life is worth a damn anyway.*

"All right, Wiseman. Lead the way."

"Excellent. My car and driver await us."

As she slipped off the stool, Sadie Levine looked past the plump lawyer through one of the diner's windows. Parked in the front of the curb was a long, black hearse. She turned and looked at Wiseman questioningly.

"Don't be alarmed," he smiled again. "It's one of the few vehicles capable of carrying my, shall we say, larger than average frame."

Frame indeed. Sadie chuckled, took another drag on her little cigar and followed Wiseman out the door.

Once inside the customized automobile, Sadie was delighted to see two heavily padded cushion-seats running the length of the interior were affixed to either side, facing each other. Wiseman plopped his massive body on the left side and Sadie took a seat on the right. His chauffeur, decked out in a professional gray outfit complete with a visored cap, closed the door behind her and then took his place behind the wheel.

Everything had happened so fast. Sadie only caught a quick glimpse of the driver but it was enough for her to recognize one of the many hoods that often frequented the Red Light district where she earned her living. Her memory pulled up the name Max Tulane. As she recalled, he was one of Topper Wyld's many gunsels. Obviously he was doing double-duty here carting Fat Jacob around town.

"Quite luxurious," the lawyer beamed, padding the purple colored seats.

"Must have cost a pretty penny," she concurred.

"Mr. Wyld never questions cost. It is one of the benefits of working for such a powerful gentlemen."

Sadie had nothing to add to that. Tulane started the big engine and smoothly drove the heavy car into the busy midday traffic.

As they drove along Sadie saw that they were moving through the rich financial heart of the city where all the fancy shops were located along with clubs, theaters and the popular radio station, WXYZ. They went several miles going northwest, then reaching the intersection with Central Avenue, Tulane took a sharp left. Twenty minutes later they came to Ocean Boulevard, a long street that started at the harbor then wound its away around most of the city before veering south until it reach Cape Noire's city limits at the Dunsdale Woods. Beyond that was interstate Highway 75.

It was at this corner that the sturdy hearse turned right and slowed down. Sadie looked back over her shoulder to see a pink, three-story Gothic Victorian set on a small slope there on the corner. Tulane took another right onto a private driveway that took them around the ornately constructed building to what had one time been a horse stable that had been converted into a three car garage. Between it and the back of the house was a huge open back lot. At the center of the building was a back door skirted by one poured cement step.

Tulane parked with the engine facing the empty garage, climbed out of hearse and rushed around the back to open the door on Wiseman's side. Sadie marveled at how the overweight attorney managed to exit the car without any difficulty whatsoever. She mentally gave him credit for what could not have been an easy maneuver. She clutched her bag, dropped her head and followed him outside.

"Thank you, Max," Wiseman nodded to his driver. "Relax for a few minutes and keep an eye out for the furniture truck. Soon as it arrives, let us know."

"Sure thing, Mr. Wiseman."

Then Wiseman waved his hands toward the back entrance. "Shall we, my dear?"

"Why the hell not," Sadie shrugged. With every passing minute her curiosity was growing. *What the hell was this all about?*

Wiseman walked to the back door while at the same time pulling a single key from a coat pocket. "I hope you don't mind our going in this back entry. I'm sure you'll understand my limitations." He pointed to the one cement step no taller than six inches. "This is a great deal more accommodating than the wooden staircase at the front."

He inserted the key in the lock, gave it a twist and easily pulled the door open. Then he took a step back to let Sadie enter first.

Sadie Levine walked into a spacious, square kitchen devoid of any furnishing except for those items required; a cast iron stove, a tall icebox and a huge white sink. Polished wooden floors shined up giving the bare room a clean pine scent. The wall opposite the back entrance had two doors. The one to the left was closed while the other on the right was opened onto a small corridor.

Fat Jacob used his cane to point at the open portal and Sadie continued towards it. Within only a few yards she emerged into an even bigger room that she surmised had to be the house's main parlor. A giant colorful Persian rug was centered in the room. Overhead a crystal chandelier hung suspended from the high ceiling. Against the left wall was a beautiful grand piano and matching stool. Atop it were scattered several sheets of paper and pens. Towards the far end was a staircase and it faced what Sadie realized was the actual front door to the well-maintained old abode.

"So what do you think of her?" Wiseman queried as he pulled the padded stool away from the piano and then carefully set his body down on it. He held his legs apart, clutching his cane in one hand while removing his hat and placing it atop the beautiful music maker.

"It's a real fancy place, that's for sure." Sadie commended. "I don't think I've ever been in a place so big...and rich."

"There are two floors above us and an attic plus a cellar. Though I'd imagine that will be turned into a delightful wine cellar eventually.

"It has six bedrooms on the second floor and four on the third. All with their own bathrooms. I would suggest you might want to make one into your office."

"What?" Sadie stopped ogling the room and returned her attention to the now smiling Jacob Wiseman. "What do you mean by that?"

Fat Jacob took a deep breath before replying. "Miss Levine, my employer, Mr. Topper Wyld wishes to make a gift of the house and the land it sits on to you."

"To me?"

Wiseman held up a hand. "Please let me finish. In return for you assisting him in turning this fine old lady into the most luxurious, glorious decorated bordello in all of Cape Noire."

"Huh? You mean a cathouse?"

"A crude term and one well suited for such houses of ill-repute that are scattered throughout our metropolis. Whereas Mr. Wyld, in his extraordinary business acumen, has seen a need for a more upscale such establishment. He wants to build a palace of sexual delights to be the home of beautiful, exotic damsels. An exclusive club that will cater only to the most influential, powerful men of our city.

"Politicians, men of industry, the cream of the elite all seeking unique, secret delights hidden from the prying eyes of the citizenry. Am I making myself clear now?"

Sadie folded her arms over her ample bosom and nodded. "Wyld wants me to be a Madam and run this fancy whorehouse you're describing. Right?"

"Bravo. Totally correct."

"So...what's the catch?"

"Catch?"

"Yeah, what does he want from me? There ain't nothing free in this world. I learned that when I was six."

Wiseman chuckled, his big stomach jumping up and down. "Miss Levine, you are a pure delight. Don't you understand? Mr. Wyld can't be bothered with the day to day management of such an enterprise. No, that will be your responsibility. And in return for your services as the new Madam, he will sign over the deed to you. It will be—for all legal purposes—yours, one hundred percent."

"And that's it?"

"Of course, Mr. Wyld will receive a percentage of whatever the house earns."

"What kind of split?"

"Sixty percent for you and your girls. On the last day of every month, his personal accountant will visit and go over your books. He will tell you what Mr. Wyld is owed. You will give him a check for that amount and as I just detailed, what is left is for you and your girls. Thus, the more successful you are, the happier all parties will be in the long run."

Sadie let Wiseman's word sink into her thoughts. It all seemed too damn good to be true, but then again, it also made perfect sense. Having lived off the streets the past ten years, she was only too aware of the various cathouses and all of them were shitholes. Which is why she'd always kept to herself and to the streets. In the kind of place Wiseman was describing, she could hire really classy girls and even get a doctor on the payroll to make sure they were kept healthy.

Then there was that kitchen she'd passed. What could a decent cook do with that? It was easy to imagine. All of it opening up a future for her she had never dreamed possible.

So what the hell? Why not give a try. All she could do is fail and then she wouldn't be any worse off than she was now.

"All right, Mr. Wiseman, I'm in. What now?"

The lawyer turned slightly on his perch and grabbed hold of the papers on the piano. "This is the deed. All you need do is sign multiple copies and the place is all yours. Also, Mr. Wyld has hired an uptown decorator who will be here in a few minutes. She's already begun buying furniture for all the various rooms. Once she arrives, she'll work with you in getting everything set up properly."

Sadie walked over to him, took up the deed and then grabbed a pen. She leaned over the piano top and scrawled her signature on the several sheets before handing them back to Wiseman. He folded them neatly and slipped them into the inner pocket of his suit coat.

"Thank you, my dear. Now that wasn't too difficult, was it?"

"I'll let you know when I wake up tomorrow, not back in my old dump. I'm still thinking this is all a foolish dream I'm having."

"Rest assured, madam. It is all very real. In fact, you might enjoy hearing your new title and getting use to it."

"Huh? What new title?"

"Why, *Madam Sadie* of course. It has a nice ring to it, don't you think?"

Sadie Levine looked around the room and smiled.

Madam Sadie. Damn, but it did have a nice ring to it.

MADAM SADIE. DAMN, BUT IT DID HAVE A NICE RING TO IT.

CHAPTER (7)

Sam Gorchen stumbled out of the Lucky Seven Emporium with a big smile on his drunken face and a fat roll of bills in his jacket pocket. A light mist had settled over the city shortly after ten p.m. and threatened rain. He pulled his wide brim fedora down tighter on his head and stood at the lip of the sidewalk looking up and down the street for a cab. The Emporium was located on a major avenue and he knew it wouldn't be long before a yellow taxi would come along.

Still the dozen or so beers he'd consumed during his several hours at the poker table were now letting him know his bladder was near to bursting. Swiveling his head around, he spotted a dark alley across the street to his right between a shoe store and a small diner. The shoe store was, of course, closed at this hour but the diner was one of those all-nighters.

Ignoring the passing cars, Sam propelled himself across the wet road. Several cars barely missed hitting him. One had to slam on its brakes and the driver rolled down his window to let his displeasure be known. "Get out of the road, moron!"

Unable to see past the glare of the headlights right atop him, Sam turned and stuck out his middle finger. "Same to you, fella." Then with a chuckle he continued on his way, oblivious to the world around him. He made it to the other sidewalk and once again stopped to make sure the alley hadn't moved during his odyssey across the street.

It had not and he quickly rushed the remaining the few yards until he was upon it. Without hesitation he entered the darkness, his left hand feeling the cement bricks that made up the shoe store's wall. Once completely away from the prying rays of the streetlamps, he turned to face that wall, hastily unbuttoned his pants and managed to achieve his desired aims.

Emptying his bladder, the tenseness in his middle-aged body relaxed. *Now that's better,* he reflected as he adjusted his pants and re-buttoned them. *Nothing like a good piss to make the world right.* Then he remembered his newly acquired guilt. *Well, maybe five hundred smackers that is.* Sam laughed and started to walk out of the alley.

It was then the scrawny looking kid with the newsboy cap materialized in front of him. They almost collided.

"Hey, look out!" Sam blurted.

The teenage boy held up his right hand to show he was holding a cigarette. "You got a light, mister?"

"Oh, sure." Sam was easily distracted. He began digging into his jacket pockets. "I got a book of matches…somewhere."

He never saw Jack Bonello silently come up behind him and in one smooth swing hit him in the back of his head with his gun. Sam dropped to the sidewalk unconscious. Tommy Bonello stuck the unlit cigarette in his mouth and then dropped to one knee to began searching through Sam Grochen's pockets.

"He dead?" Jack asked, sliding the .38 Police Special back in his belt.

"How the hell do I know?" Tommy mumbled, tossing out pieces of papers and loose change he'd found. "I ain't no doctor. 'Sides…who cares." Then his fingers took hold of the roll of bills in their victim's jacket pocket. When he pulled it out a smile blossomed on his face.

"BINGO!"

"How much is there?"

Tommy stood, tore off the rubber band and hastily counted the bills. Most were twenties and tens. "Holy shit, Jack. Five hundred clams!" He held them so his twin could get a better look.

Jack grabbed the stash, carefully divided it and then handed Tommy his half.

"Want to stick around and see if we can nail another one," Tommy suggested, shoving his two-fifty in his pocket.

"Nah," Jack disagreed. "Why push our luck? Come on, let's go find a diner and get something to eat. I'm hungry."

"All right."

As they started down the street, Tommy threw one arm around Jack's shoulder, pulled the cigarette out of his mouth and grinned. "Hey, Jack. You got a light?"

Saul's Pool Parlor was filled with its regulars by ten p.m. The bar area was crowded with three harried waitresses running back and forth between the dozen round tables filled with drinking men and women, and the long bar where Jerry Conklin and Dan Pardee were on the move constantly filling drink orders and handling those folks seated before them on the round cushioned stools. In the back half of the large room were six billiard tables and all were in constant use. Supervising all this activity, seated on a three foot platform set against the back wall, was owner Saul Chevesky; a short fellow with a bushy gray beard, bulbous round nose and bald head. Next to his chair was a small table on which stood a half-empty bottle of rye whiskey, a small glass and a brass ashtray filled with cigar ash. The remainder of the stogie was still lodged in his mouth. With his beard surrounding it, the smoking cigar looked like a mini canon tip protruding from a thick forest of gray hair.

The platform chair was Saul's throne from which he would sit and contentedly survey his little domain every night. A congenial sort, he bantered amiably with his customers, many he'd known for years. On occasions he would accept a challenge to play a round at the tables. Saul was known for running the boards and few dared bet against him in a game of nine ball.

Thick cigarette and cigar smoke filled the place like a low hanging cloud and the chatter of a hundred voices was a symphony to the human condition. It was a typical night unfolding in Cape Noire until the front door banged open and in walked the tall redhead with a black patch over her left eye.

Susie Cummings, one of the three waitresses, spotted her first and hurried to the bar to tell Dan and Jerry.

Betty One-Eye was six feet four inches of lean, hard-packed Irish muscle. She wore men's clothing, from heavy work boots to black pants and matching shirt over which was draped a dark gray trench coat she kept unbuttoned. Her orange-colored hair was tied into a severe ponytail that fell to the small of her back. Rumor had it that woven into its tip were razor blades she would use to lethal efficiency when whipping her head about turning the two-foot extension into her own scorpion's sting.

Beatrice Ann McCauley, as she'd been christened at birth, was well known throughout the city as Big Swede Jorgenson's chief enforcer. When Big Swede wanted a job done, he sent Betty One-Eye.

Behind her were two rough looking bruisers; one was black and the other yellow. Built like a tank on two legs, Eli St. Jonah was the product of the ghetto streets of Little Jamaica located at the northeast end of town. His partner, Bulok Que, was an immigrant sailor of Mongolian descent who wore his greasy black hair down to his shoulders and possessed two beady little black eyes like those of a ferret.

All three were killers. Of that there was no question.

The second Susie alerted the bartenders of their arrival, Jerry lifted his cleaning rag and waved it at his boss to get his attention. It took several repetitions before Chevesky saw the signal and acknowledged it with a wave of his hand. At that Jerry pointed to the trio now making their way past the bar. At their sight, Saul Chevesky pulled the cigar from his mouth and sat up straighter in his chair.

Betty One-Eye continued on past the bar giving both Dan and Jerry a cursory look, well aware each of them most likely had shotguns under the counter and knew how to use them. She smiled to herself and headed toward the pool tables with St. Jonah and Que on her heels like well-trained pets. As the trio moved along, players stopped their activity and watched them with understandable apprehension. Betty's reputation was one of blood and mayhem and she rarely made social calls.

"Betty," Chevesky said, loud enough to be heard over the din of voices. "What a pleasant surprise. To what do I owe the pleasure of this unexpected visit?"

Betty stood before his platform and looked up at him with a mischievous grin on her face. It was actually a quite pretty face even with the leather patch covering her left eye. The right one was a vibrant green now completely focused on Saul Chevesky.

"Oh, please, Saul," she chuckled. "Surely you can guess why I'm here."

"Ah," he motioned with the cigar in his hands. "Is this about Big Swede's recent offer to buy my little enterprise?"

"It is. He's most anxious to hear if you've come to a decision yet?"

Chevesky stuck the cigar back in his mouth and puffed on it for several seconds. Smoke curled up in front of his face almost hiding it. When it had wafted away he was smiling. "As much as his offer was overly generous, I'm afraid I'm going to have to decline." He swept his arms out as if to embrace the place. "I've come to think of this is my home and I guess I just don't want to leave it."

"Aw, that's a shame," Betty frowned. "You see, Mr. Jorgenson simply cannot accept that answer."

"Oh, really?" Chevesky stood up, removed the stogie from his lips and snarled. "And what's he going to do about it? Take it from me?"

Betty One-Eye folded her hands in front of coat. Behind her she guessed the bartenders were now reaching for their concealed weapons. The tension in the room was increasing rapidly.

"You know, Saul," she turned away from him slowly. "It has always puzzled me why people have to make things hard on themselves." She walked up to a cue rack mounted to the wall to right of the platform and casually removed one of the sticks. "I mean, you stood to make a lot of money off this shithole. Much more than it's really worth. And yet you say no."

She returned to the spot before the now irate Chevesky and looking up at him, shook her head slightly. "No, Saul. Mr. Jorgenson isn't going to take it from you..."

Betty One-Eye brought up her right leg, shoved the cue stick down and broke it in two ragged-edged pieces.

"...I am."

Then before anyone realized her intent, she stepped up on the platform and shoved the ripped end of the smaller half into Chevesky's throat embedding it three inches deep. Saul's cigar fell from his mouth, his eyes widened in shock as blood came gushing from the area around the wooden stake.

Chevesky's hands grabbed at the stake in his throat but his fingers slipped because of the blood covering it. His knees buckled and he collapsed, knocking over the small table next to his chair. The platform shook from the impact of his body.

Someone in the room behind Betty screamed.

Both barkeeps began to pull out their shotguns.

Bulok Que spun around at the same time, drawing a long dagger from beneath his coat. In one smooth motion he flipped it in the air, caught the needle sharp tip with his fingers and then hurled it across the room. The knife hit Jerry Conklin in the heart surprising the life out of him. He looked down at blade protruding from his chest and then simply collapsed.

More screams from the ladies.

At the sight of his co-worker's fate, Dan Pardee dropped his own shotgun and threw his hands up high and yelled, "I give up!"

It was a smart move as Eli St. Jonas was now pointing a long-barreled Colt revolver at him.

Betty One-Eye smiled and motioned her man to lower his gun. He nodded and did as ordered. Betty then clapped her hands loudly to address the still shaken customers.

"As of now, this place is under new management, that being Mr. Swede Jorgenson. Now, if anyone goes to the cops about what happened here, I would suggest they also take out a new life insurance policy.

"Do I make myself clear, people?"

Frozen faces looked back at her.

"Good. Now all of you, except for the staff, get the hell out of here. NOW!"

Instantly chairs were pushed back, remaining beers downed in gulps and hats grabbed as the crowd jumped to their feet and rushed chaotically to the door. A few women were shoved around until their respective male companions held on to their arms and guided them along through the front door. In under two minutes, the only six people left in the parlor were the three waitresses, Dan Pardee, Betty One-Eye and her two henchmen, Bulok Que and Eli St. John.

Betty surveyed the room for a second, then dropped off the platform and marched to the door. She opened it, looked out and said, in a loud voice. "All clear, sir."

An anxious Dan Pardee and his frightened three waitresses watched as the tall, beautiful killer stepped back to allow her employer to enter.

Big Swede Jorgenson was Betty's equal in height, though in his fancy topcoat and homburg hat, he was a much more commanding presence. He looked at the near empty pool emporium and then turning to Betty, reached out a gloved hand and touched her cheek gently.

"You never fail me, Betty."

"Thanks, Boss." She started to blush. Big Swede was perhaps the only man she had ever admired and considered her better. "Me and the boys were just doing our job."

"Yes, but you do it so wonderfully, dear girl," he quibbled with a smile on his tanned, long face adorned with bushy white eyebrows that matched the thick wavy hair on his head. He continued into the room followed by four other men, all of the same caliber as St. John and Que; criminal thugs who would march into Hades at the snap of his fingers.

Jorgenson went over to the body of Saul Chevesky. He removed his hat and holding it with two hands, glared down at the still warm corpse with a disapproving look. "Tsk, tsk, Saul. You could have made this all so easy and walked away a happy man. Now you're nothing but worm food, you poor pathetic fool."

He replaced the expensive, custom-made hat on his head while making a wry grimace. "Such is business, I suppose."

The powerful Cape Noire crime lord then approached the bar and scrutinized Dan Pardee with a critical glare.

"What's your name, son?"

"Dan Pardee, Mr. Jorgenson."

"So, you know who I am do you?"

"Of course, sir. Everyone knows who you are."

That last bit amused Jorgenson. He slowly peeled off the rich kid gloves on his hands and smiled. "Tell me, Dan. Could you manage this operation if I offered you the position?"

Surprised by the question, Pardee bit down on his lower lip and scratched the back of his head. "Geez, I guess so, sir. I've been here a few years now and it's not that hard a job to run a place like this."

"As I've already surmised," Jorgenson agreed. "How much was Saul paying you per week?"

"A hundred dollars."

"I'll pay you a thousand a week to be my manager and run the joint. How's that sound to you?"

"Ah…it sounds great, Mr. Jorgenson."

"Good, then we shake on it." He extended his right hand.

Pardee took it and Big Swede squeeze tightly. "Keep it running smoothly and we'll have no problems. Understood, Dan?"

"Yes, sir, I do." He could feel the bones in his hand about to break. "I swear."

"Excellent." Jorgenson let him go and then pointed to the waitresses. "And give them all a raise too. I want only happy employees. Get the place cleaned up and looking good. I want it to make me a lot of money."

"I'll do my best," Dan Pardee vowed.

"I'm sure you will, son," Jorgenson chuckled happily. "I'm sure you will."

CHAPTER (8)

Sitting by herself in her richly decorated, massive suite, Alexis Wyld reflected for the hundredth time that evening on how much she truly hated school work. It was a month since her mother's passing and household activity had returned to what passed for routine in the ornate, expansive mansion with all its rooms. They were laid out on three floors; not to forget the elaborate cellar and cavernous attic that spanned the entire length of the building. Alexis was positive the attic was a haven for blood-sucking bats and she rarely dared venture into it alone. Oh, once or twice she'd gone up with Mrs. Awsmane, the matronly housekeeper who managed the staff made up of three maids and a Parisian trained chef named Henri. The spacious top floor enclave was filled with trunks, unused cabinets, and other discarded furnishing that every once in a while were needed by Mrs. Awsmane for a specific duty. Alexis had ventured along out of curiosity and after a few trips determined that was all she wanted to know about that dusty grand attic.

Alexis' room was located on the eastern corner of the second floor so that every morning bright rays of the new day's sun would splash up against four windows bathing her room in a magnificent, warm glow. All well and good when there was sun. On dark and rainy days, the space felt more like a prison cell to her. As it did this particular evening as she sat at her desk to the right of the hall door brooding over some boring facts about European history.

Who gave a damn about what happened in Europe long ago? She reasoned logically. *I mean, this is America. Why should we give a shit about what happened over there?* Even thinking the word shit made her giggle a little. She could easily imagine her father's reaction if that word, or any other such language, ever escaped her mouth. Topper Wyld was always the proper gentlemen and she had never once heard him utter a foul word. Alexis was by no means naïve about her father. She was well aware; thanks to the newspaper articles some of her girlfriends had shared with her, that her loving father was considered a very powerful business man who many believed dealt in illegal enterprises.

Which, she knew, made him a criminal. But that was also not her concern. At twelve, the pretty brunette with the dark eyes was primarily interested in one thing. Well maybe two; boys and sex. In fact that's all her little clique at the Lincoln Avenue Grade School ever talked about. It was as if the world revolved around the biological changes puberty was putting all of them through. Alexis thought of Nancy Cabot already having noticeable breasts making her the envy of all the other girls; never mind she'd began her menstrual cycle months earlier as well. Alexis and the others simply couldn't hide their jealousy. It was obvious, when walking through the school corridors, Nancy would make certain her chest was pushed forward catching the eye of every single boy in their classes. It was terribly wicked and again she wished her own body would start to change faster.

It just wasn't fair; Alexis pushed away from her desk and went over to the full length mirror in her bathroom. Dressed in a plaid skirt, white sox and a silk blouse, she posed before her reflection by putting one hand on her hip. She took a pose she had seen in glamour magazines used by sultry, alluring models. Sadly, all she saw was an awkward little girl trying to be a woman and she stuck her tongue out at the other Alexis.

Unable to quell her frustrations a minute longer, Alexis left her room, extinguishing the lights as she did so. If she was going to go exploring this late in the evening, she didn't need anyone, particularly her father, catching her at it. Thus she moved over the carpeted hall floor like a stalking cat. There was only one light aglow on the second floor as usual and that was the one over the staircase landing. As Alexis moved along the wooden railing that overlooked the first floor foyer, she could hear voices coming from her father's den/office located beneath her towards the rear of the mansion.

Earlier in the evening she'd looked out her window to see a familiar black hearse pull up the circular driveway and recognized it as belonging to her father's business advisor, Attorney Jacob Wiseman. She was aware her father's men called him Fat Jacob behind his back because of his obesity. Alexis often imagined him as a gross real-life Humpty Dumpty and wondered what would happen if he were to actually take a tumble off a high precipice. *Ooh, that would be so icky.*

Quickly dispelling such a disgusting image from her mind, Alexis continued past the stairs onto the west section of the second floor where her nanny, Yvette Minault's quarters were to be found. She knew the rooms would be empty, as after dinner, Yvette had asked her father if his man, Harry Beest, could take her into the city to do some shopping. Her father agreed and the ruggedly handsome assistant arrived an hour later just as the lovely Miss Minault was helping Alexis with her homework schedule. Yvette promised she'd go over the completed assignments with her charge at breakfast the next morning before she went off to school. Then she was gone with the debonair Mr. Beest.

Alexis thought he was very good looking, in a rough kind of way. Anyway, with Miss Minault gone for at least a few hours, it would give the inquisitive girl time to explore the woman's clothes and make up. Yvette was always so chic, Alexis was eager to go through her closet and see what other elegant dresses might be stored in there. As she reached the door, she looked about the darkened corridor one last time, then twisted the knob and entered.

"Ah, this brandy is superb," Jacob Wiseman commented as he ran the tiny glass snifter under his nose. He beamed at his host, Topper Wyld, and then he took a sip slowly savoring the exquisite flavor.

"I have a shipment sent from Paris once every few months," Wyld said, as he put the bottle down on his desk. Dressed in casual clothes and evening dinner jacket, he was standing in front of the desk while Wiseman sat on the gray loveseat set against the wall to the right of the desk. It was the only piece of furniture that could accommodate his bulk.

Wyld leaned back against his desk and folded his arms over his chest wanting to get back to their initial conversation. "And the affair at the pool hall two weeks ago; what was that all about? Is Big Swede starting to get too big?"

Fat Jacob smacked his lips after finishing his brandy and wiped them with a silk handkerchief. "Perhaps, but I really don't think so. Remember, Chevesky's sits squarely in neutral territory in regards to both your mutual interests."

Wyld tugged at his chin. "I am well aware of our agreed upon boundaries, Jacob."

"And Big Swede has clearly respected them for the quite some time now," the lawyer felt the need to remind his partner. "My thinking is this was simply a minor expansion of his little kingdom."

"Understood," Wyld grudgingly agreed. "But Cape Noire is not a limitless piece of dirt. According to my sources, we currently have eight different outfits operating within several blocks of each other."

"And you don't like that." Wiseman was all too aware of Wyld's ambitions.

"Of course not. It's sloppy. Gambling, smuggling, drugs, prostitution are all lucrative businesses, but they are being horribly mismanaged." Wyld began to pace, his hands now clasped behind his back as he continued to rant. "It seems like every week there's a new gun battle somewhere in the city and as a result operations get disrupted for all of us."

"Well, that's only understandable," Wiseman held out his empty sniffer. "After all, even our corrupt police officials have to make a show of enforcing the law if only to placate the good and decent people who live here."

Wyld stopped his pacing, picked up the brandy decanter and went over to refill his advisor's glass. "I still don't like it, Jacob. If I ran the city, things would be a whole lot better. More efficient…for everyone."

"I won't argue that," Wiseman took another sip of the sweet elixir. "But considering all the other things you are involved with now, I don't think this is the time to be challenging the other bosses."

"Hmm, you may be right." Wyld grabbed another snifter off the cabinet behind his desk and poured himself a shot of brandy. "All right, let's move on here." He went around his desk and sat down. He took a drink and allowed himself to relax.

"How's the new bordello coming along."

"Very well," Wiseman smiled happily. "Far better than we'd hoped. I'm quite pleased with Miss Levine; she is proving to be a very astute business woman and in the past few months has recruited a dozen very comely and desirable young ladies."

"Excellent. How soon before it is ready to open?"

"No more than a week or so."

"Good. I've received a few calls from friends at City Hall who are most anxious to sample the house's delights."

"Trust me, Topper. They will not be disappointed."

"Good. There's one other matter I wish to discuss."

"And that is?"

"I've been receiving reports about two young boys wreaking havoc in the dock districts."

"Really?"

"Yes. Harry heard they are wanted for shooting a cop, among other petty crimes."

"Oh, my." Wiseman put a hand over his heart. "That is dramatic isn't it."

"Call it what you will, I want to know more about them. Use whatever snitches you have in that area and find out what you can."

"Of course, I'll put in a few calls to the nearest precinct and see what it's all about. Any particular reason you have an interest in two wild street urchins?"

"Oh, nothing concrete," Topper Wyld wondered aloud. "I'm just curious. I mean, killing a cop takes balls. I want to meet these boys and see if they're the real deal. Who knows, maybe I might have a need for them. Never too soon to start recruiting new soldiers. Eh, Jacob?"

"But of course, old friend. You are right as always."

Meanwhile, Alexis Wyld sat in front of the vanity mirror in Yvette Minault's room enthusiastically examining her array of cosmetic applications. For a young girl, finding a table top filled with only the finest powders, lipstick tubes and eye make-up was akin to an early Christmas surprise from Santa. Assured her nanny wouldn't be home for another few hours, the mischievous Alexis had turned on the lights when entering the bedroom and was now gleefully about to try several of the beauty products starting with the various lipsticks.

There were four on the table ranging from a very soft, delicate pink to one offering a very bold, cheery red color. Feeling naughty, she uncapped the bright red one and puckering her full lips at the mirror, Alexis carefully applied the sticky paste. She smacked her lips carefully as she did so until they were both covered completely. Then she sat up a little straighter on the padded stool and turned her head slightly from side to side, smiling coyly as she did so.

"Hello, Harry," she said, acting out an imaginary scenario in her imagination. "What do you think of this color? You approve. Why, how charming. Maybe if you're nice, I'll let you taste my warm and inviting lips."

Now I'm sounding like one of those floozies in the cheap romantic magazines the maids have stashed in the kitchen. She giggled at her own silliness.

Looking away from the lighted mirror, her eyes fell on the bureau to the left of the large clothes closet. Alexis swiveled around on the stool, got to her feet and approached the bureau. Atop the rich teak wood were a few jewelry boxes, ceramic statuettes of small ballerinas molded in white porcelain with touches of gold luster paint. Everything was neatly arranged and Alexis was careful not to pick up anything and accidently rearrange things so that Yvette would know someone had been in her room.

The bureau had three drawers which she carefully opened one at a time. The first contained blouses, scarves, shawls and cotton shirts. The second was filled with delicate undergarments; slips, panties, stockings and brassieres. Alexis held up one of the bras. It was made of satin and colored a light blue. Just the cups themselves evidenced what she already knew about her nanny; Yvette was more than fully developed in the bosom department. Finally the bottom draw revealed more intimate apparel, only these clearly intended for more than sleeping as the seamed silk stockings were a smoky black color and next to them was a red garter belt adorned with embroidered roses. Then she found the black opera gloves and strapless half-cut bra.

She could clearly envision the lovely Miss Minault in such a scandalous outfit. Maybe her nanny wasn't the stiff-necked prude she thought her to be. That made Alexis smile. *We all do have our little secrets, don't we?*

She wrapped the skimpy bra about her own chest and was starting back to the vanity mirror to see how she looked in it when she heard the voices from out in the hall. Alexis stopped in mid-step. The voices were getting closer and louder.

She recognized Yvette's light musical laugh and knew she had to hide. Spinning around, she went back to bureau, dropped the bra into it and quietly slid the drawer shut. Then frantically surveying the room, she made her decision. Going under the bed was stupid. Something she might have done as a child. But now that was out of the question and she bolted for the only remaining logical sanctuary; the closet. Alexis opened the door and dashed inside stumbling among the hanging dresses. She nearly tripped over the row of shoes lined up on the inside floor. Hastily she closed the door behind her just as she heard the front door swing open behind her.

"Oh," Yvette Minault uttered upon entering her boudoir followed by a jovial Harry Beest; his arms filled with several colorful bags.

"Oh, what?" he asked, almost bumping into her from behind.

"I thought I'd shut off the light when I left earlier."

Beest looked around nonchalantly and shrugged. "You must have just forgotten is all. I do it all the time."

Peeling off her white cotton gloves and stylish cloche hat, Minault nodded. "Perhaps you are right. I've just been so busy lately; I suppose I could have rushed out without shutting them off."

"You were obviously distracted by the thought of spending time with me," Beest suggested brazenly.

"Harry, you're too much."

"I already know that, Dollface." He held up the bags in his hands. "What do you want me to do with these?"

"Oh, just throw them in the closet. I'll go through them later."

Alexis's heart almost stopped beating. She pushed herself to one side of the door and dove behind as many hanging dresses as she could while silently praying she wouldn't be found out. The door swung open and she saw Harry Beest's arms reach in and simply dropped the three big paper bags onto the row of shoes. Alexis held her breath. Then the door was closed again and she nearly collapsed with relief, her lungs starting up again.

That was too close.

"There you go, Miss Minault. All set."

"My, my, how formal you are. Well, then, Mr. Beest, how can I thank you for traipsing all over with me this evening?"

"Oh, I'm sure you can find a way, Dollface."

When Beest's question went unanswered for a long moment, curiosity got the best of Alexis and she carefully wiggled her way back to the front of the closet. Then very, very slowly holding the steel handle in her hands, she cracked the door open by a half-inch. Just enough so that she could peek out with her left eye.

The reason her nanny hadn't responded was because she was in Harry Beest's embrace and they were kissing passionately. Or at least what looked to be passionately to the still inexperienced Alexis. But it was still clear to her that their kiss was something more than simply a little peck with two sets of lips touching. They were pushing their bodies against each other wantonly and Beest's hands, from what she could see, were moving up and down Minault's backside focused primarily on her rounded derriere. Their kiss seemed to go on forever, until their slobbering noises told Alexis she was witnessing what her schoolmates called 'french kissing' wherein tongues were shoved into another's mouth.

Ewww! Still she did not stop watching from her hiding spot.

Beest was clearly feverish in his grasping affection of the nubile Miss Minault. Once their kiss had broken, he began fondling her ripe breasts through her blouse and threatened to rip it off her.

"No," she breathed heavily pushing him back. "Not like that. Go, put out the light and come to the bed."

As Harry Beest turned to comply with the lovely brunette's command, she went over to the lamp on the table by her bed and switched it on. With an audible click, the overhead light went out and now the only illumination came from the small lamp. Beest returned to Minault only to have her avoid his arms and move around him.

"No, Harry. Please. Sit on the bed and let me do this for you."

For a second he seemed puzzled by her request. Then she began unbuttoning her blouse and he smiled knowingly. Removing his own suit jacket, he tossed it on the floor.

Upon seeing his automatic in its leather shoulder rig, the nubile young temptress pointed to it chuckling. "Ooh, I don't think you'll have any need of that big gun, Harry. I'm really not dangerous."

He went to the bed, sat on it and easily unhooked the holster setting it and the automatic it held beside the lamp. "I'm not so sure about that, Sweetie."

Yvette Minault laughed and continued to strip for him. With the last button undone, she let the blouse slide off her shoulders and fall to her feet. Beest took off his tie, kicked off his shoes and stretched out with his back against the bed's headboard, his eyes remaining fixed on the seductive nanny.

Minault easily unzipped her tight skirt and stepped out of it leaving her wearing only her black high heel shoes, panties and bra.

"Like what you see, Harry?" she inquired wickedly, as her hands reached behind her back to find the bra's metal clasp.

In the closet, Alexis almost gasped aloud as she heard Yvette coyly tease Harry Beest in almost the exact same fashion she'd only just played out in her mind minutes earlier while seated before the vanity mirror.

"Oh yeah, Dollface. I like every single inch of it."

With abandon, Miss Minault flung her bra away and joined him on the bed. She and Beest once again kissed but only briefly this time. He firmly took hold of her shoulders, held her tightly while his lust-filled gaze looked on her perfect breasts. Then he brought his mouth to one of them and began to suck it greedily. Yvette's head tiled back as she squealed in pleasure.

"Oh, God, yes, Harry. Kiss me all over."

Alexis Wyld couldn't turn away, watching the two adults caught up in the heat of sexual desire. She was mesmerized as Beest continued to cover the woman's body with his lips and hands, making her cry out with what she assumed was sheer physical delight. And as the two lovers progressed, her own blood began to race through her veins. She felt an odd tingle between her legs and slowly pushed down on it with the palm of her right hand.

Oh...that feels so good.

So good she couldn't stop.

For the next three hours Alexis watched and waited as her nanny and her father's bodyguard made arduous love several times; each more consuming then their previous bout. They were like insatiable animals. All of which stirred feelings in the girl she had only ever read about in those cheap romance titles. Still, it was late by the time the heavy breathing couple turned off the light and went to sleep exhausted from their sexual antics.

Wanting to be certain they were both fast in slumberland, Alexis waited even longer in her hideaway, all the while doing her best to fight off her

ALEXIS WYLD COULDN'T TURN AWAY WATCHING...

own drowsiness. Falling asleep in the closet now would be the end of her for sure. Finally, when she simply couldn't put it off any longer, she gently took hold of the handle and carefully pushed the door open. She exited the closet, closed the door and tip-toed to the bedroom door. She could barely see anything as the room was lost to her in the darkness. Her only guide was the thin light from the hall visible at the door's bottom.

Reaching it, she once again held her breath, grasped the knob and quietly opened the door. One of the hinges made a tiny squeaky noise and she froze. She looked back over her shoulder to the bed where she was praying the sound hadn't disturbed the unconscious pair under the sheets. When there was no activity, she sighed, moved out into the hall and delicately pulled the door shut. That done, she swiftly raced away down the hall.

While back in the bedroom, a fully awake Harry Beest put his gun back down on the lamp table. In his line of work, Beest couldn't afford to be anything but a light sleeper. Thus the second Alexis Wyld had emerged from the closet, he'd awakened fully alert and silently taken his pistol from its holster. Moving slowly, he'd turned his head towards the door as Alexis's form was outlined by the hall light.

He was amused at the thought that Wyld's mischievous daughter had been in the closet all the time he and Minault had been screwing. It was all too funny. *And she thinks she got away with it,* he reasoned lowering his head back on the pillow. *Gonna have to keep a closer eye on that little birdie from now on.*

He quickly fell back to sleep.

CHAPTER (9)

After the first few weeks of working at the Gridiron Saloon, Butch Hammer settled into his new routine easily. He liked the busy atmosphere of the bar with all its patrons, both the regular locals and the many sailors from far off foreign lands. The noise, the smoke from too many cigarettes and cigars, all contributed to a pulsing beat that suited his congenial nature. It didn't matter if he was in the kitchen making up sandwiches or behind the bar working alongside the colorful Molly McCoy. He liked the bar and quickly came to accept it as his new home.

Like most such establishments in Cape Noire, midweek was always the slowest and this particular Wednesday night was no different. Soon after eight o'clock, seeing they only had a dozen or so customers, Molly had taken off her apron and tossed it at him. "Gonna call it a night, Butch. You and Peggy can handle things without me."

Her daughter Peggy was in fact seated at the bar sipping on a beer. That's how slow the place really was.

"So, you gonna go relax in a hot tub?" Hammer suggested.

"Yes siree," the square shaped, one-time Irish immigrant concurred. "Then I'm gonna put on my slippers, pour myself a shot of whiskey and sit down and listen to the radio. They got some dandy music shows this time of night."

"Sounds like a nice way to end the day," Hammer approved.

"Damn straight." McCoy walked around the bar and passing Peggy as she headed for the back stairs to the apartments above, she cocked an eyebrow. "You two behave now."

"Ha," her daughter laughed. "Get out of here, will ya."

Molly McCoy patted Peggy's shoulder and was soon gone.

"What was that all about?" Hammer asked, as he picked up a small tub full of glasses to carry back into the kitchen for cleaning.

"Aw, Ma has it in her head that maybe you and I should get together." Peggy dropped off her stool and started around the end of the long bar.

Turning to the kitchen doorway, the ex-boxer was surprised by her remark. "You're kidding, right?"

"No, I'm not, Butch."

In the back room, Hammer put down the tub and started filling the steel sink with hot water and soap. Peggy stopped at the door and leaned against the frame.

"Oh," was all he could think to say at the moment. Peggy McCoy was pretty and he had to admit, every now and then he'd look at her and wonder what would happen if he ever got the gumption to ask her out.

"So what do you say, Butch? Would you like to take me to a picture-show some night?"

"Huh?" He shut off the water tap and turned to face her, hands on his hips. "Are you asking me out on a date?"

"Of course I am, you blockhead. Figured if I waited for you to ask me, hell would freeze over first." And then she smiled and Butch Hammer was more than just a happy man.

"Well, okay. It's a date. We're going to see a flicker. But when...and who's gonna help Molly if both of us are gone at the same time?"

Before Peggy could answer, they both heard the front door open and she turned to see who was coming in. Looking over her shoulder, she said, "We'll get back to that in a minute."

Seeing her leave, Hammer rushed over to get a peek at who had entered. The last people he expected to see where two coppers. One was in full blue uniform while his partner had on a trenchcoat and brown snap brim fedora.

"Yo, Terry," Peggy McCoy greeted as the two lawmen stepped up and took stools side by side. "What's got you out and about at this late hour of the night?"

Officer Terrence Deusault removed his cap and set it on the bar. "We're chasing down a couple of street rats, Peggy. Twin boys calling themselves…"

"The Bone Brothers," she interrupted. "No meaner pair of rascals ever walked the streets of Cape Noire."

"You know them, Miss?" The handsome fellow in civilian clothes spoke up.

Officer Deusault made the introductions. "Peggy McCoy, meet Detective Dan Rains. He's new to the precinct."

"Nice to meet you," she nodded. "And yes, to answer your question, but only by reputation. Why the big hassle now?"

"We believe they murdered a policeman two weeks ago and are now committing robberies all over this part of town."

"I see. Can I get you boys anything to drink?"

Officer Deusault frowned. "Peggy, we're still on duty."

"I meant coffee."

"Oh. Sure, I'd like a cup."

"Yeah, why not," Detective Rains chimed in. "My feet are killing me and they need a little rest."

There was a fresh pot behind her on the bottom liquor shelf and she filled two big mugs with the hot brew. She spotted Butch Hammer at the door and winked at him to let him know everything was okay. He smiled and went back into the kitchen to finish his glass washing task.

Setting the two white mugs before the coppers, she explained, "Sorry, but we don't have any cream or sugar."

"S'all right, black is fine by me," Rains picked up his mug.

"Likewise," Officer Deusault echoed. He took a cautious sip. It was strong coffee just the way he liked it.

"So exactly how are these little devils operating?" Peggy McCoy asked out of curiosity.

"Well, they've established a kind of pattern," Rains told her. "Seems they stake out some night spot, a club, dance hall or casino and then wait for some guy leaving drunk as a skunk and then they mug him. Victims are so soused, they don't have a clue what's happening until it's all over and they're lots of dollars poorer."

"Fascinating." The redhead bit her lower lip. "You say they target nightclubs."

"Yes."

"I wonder, have they hit anyone at the Gray Owl?"

"Excuse me?" Rains looked from Peggy to Officer Deusault. "The Gray Owl? What's that?"

"Only the swankiest casino in town," Deusault replied. "It's owned by Big Swede Jorgenson." He looked back at Peggy. "And now that you mention it, the brothers haven't hit it…"

Detective Rains finished his sentence for him. "…yet."

Waldo Dunzinger opened the front door to a glorious warm day. He looked down and saw the morning paper on the bottom step. It was folded up and tied with a thick rubber band. He looked down the street in time to see the neighborhood paperboy, Petey Adams, wheeling away on his red bicycle, his canvas pouch hung over his left shoulder. Waldo watched the lad moving past another house; reach into the pouch with his right hand, grab another copy and then with a graceful throw hurl it through the air. By the time the missile hit its stoop target, Petey was turning onto another street.

Such was the agile dexterity of youth, Waldo mused as he bent over and picked up the Professor's newspaper. Going down the main hall to the kitchen, he wondered what it would have been like to have had a bike. To the best of his memories, he'd never even ridden one before. *Probably fall off it now and break something,* he thought wryly. Truth was that there didn't exist a bike strong enough to handle his size and weight.

Professor Bugosi, dressed in his white laboratory smock, was almost finished with his usual breakfast of eggs and bacon when Waldo entered the kitchen. Beside his plate were several journals in which the scientist was already scribbling.

"Ah, the paper," Bugosi looked up as Waldo handed it to him. "Thank you, Waldo. May I have another cup of coffee?"

"Sure thing, Professor." Waldo took the still warm pot off the stove and refilled Bugosi's cup and then his own. He'd already eaten earlier, as was his habit, before preparing his employer's morning fare.

Pushing aside his journals, Bugosi pulled off the rubber band and unfolded the paper. Across the top was a three inch banner proclaiming, GANGLAND VIOLENCE EXPLODES. He drank some coffee and then tapped the paper with his forefinger.

"Stupid fools revel in destroying each other, Waldo. It's so ludicrous. But then again, it all plays into our hands doesn't it?"

Waldo had no clue what his boss meant and merely grunted.

"Ah, never mind, my friend," Bugosi continued. "It will all become clear to you as time goes on. You see, people like Topper Wyld and his associates, by the illegal nature of their enterprises will come to appreciate the things I can provide them with. The very tools in which to wage their petty little wars and defeat their rivals."

"If you say so, Professor. Say, you got any errands for me to run today?"

"A few. I'll need you to pick up some supplies at the electronics store later. I've reached the end of phase one on the transformation process, I'm also going to need a new subject to work with."

"You want me to get another dog?"

"No, Waldo. This time I'm going to need a human subject."

"Huh? You mean a person?"

"Yes. Will that be a problem?"

"Ah, I don't know." Waldo scratched his large chin. "Geez, Professor. That ain't like just grabbing a mutt off the streets."

Bugosi pushed back his chair and walked around the table to face his tall assistant. "I would imagine there's not much difference when you examine the situation. Consider all the derelicts lying on the streets in the poor areas of our commonwealth. Aren't they much like the loose mongrels you've been collecting?"

"You mean the bums and winos."

"Exactly." Bugosi smacked Waldo on the arm. "That's exactly what I mean. Lost souls no one will ever miss. Men who contribute nothing to society. How difficult would it be for you to procure one of these...ah... winos as you call them?"

"Probably not hard at all, if I was to offer them a drink. Those guys will do anything for booze."

"And there you have it my boy. After nightfall, you'll set out on your task and scour the docks and back alleys. I'm sure it won't take you long to find us a subject."

"No, I guess not, Professor."

"Good, then it's settled." Bugosi went to collect his journals and return to his upstairs labs. At the hall door he turned and smiled at Waldo. "And think of it like this. Whoever it is you bring us, that poor chap will finally be able to contribute to something great to the world other than his own measly existence."

"Ah…what?"

"Science, my boy. Our lost soul will be a true pioneer of science. Now that's a distinct and unique honor."

Professor Bugosi exited leaving Waldo to mull over what he'd just been told. He couldn't say he was happy with the idea, but then again the boss was the boss and he didn't want to jeopardize his job.

He set about cleaning the kitchen and stopped thinking about things beyond his control.

Harry Beest came down the mansion stairs adjusting his tie. It was just after seven a.m. He saw that Topper Wyld's office door was open. Which was no surprise as the boss was an early riser and didn't like to waste time. Every day was a well planned out series of events that had to be meticulously adhered to. Beest was almost at the open door when Wyld emerged, a stuffed manila folder in his hands. As ever, he was impeccably dressed. He looked up and saw his number one man.

"Ah, Harry, there you are."

"Morning, Mr. Wyld."

"Have you had breakfast yet?"

"No, sir. Just woke up twenty minutes ago."

"Then come join me. Chef Louis is putting together bacon and eggs and blueberry muffins."

"Sounds delicious."

As he walked beside the smaller Wyld, Beest glanced at the folder. "Got a busy day planned out, sir?"

"Yes, Harry. With some important meetings along the way."

They entered the spacious square dining room at the same time as the chef, a beefy fellow with a thin gray mustache who was pushing a food tray in from the opposite door to the kitchen located in the back of the house.

"Ah, just in time, Mr. Wyld."

Wyld looked down at the several covered trays and took a sniff. "Hmm, smells heavenly, Louis." He nodded to Beest. "Mr. Beest will be joining me this morning."

"Excellent," the Chef clapped his hands together. "Please, take your seats and help yourselves while I go and get the coffee."

Wyld lifted up the lid off the first plate to reveal half a dozen fried eggs alongside twice as many long strips of dark crispy bacon. The second tray held buttered toast and a dozen fat, still warm blueberry muffins.

"Here, let me," Beest offered grabbing the serving tongs as Wyld took the chair at the head of the table. He then picked up Wyld's plate and indicated the hot food. "What'll it be, boss?"

Spreading a napkin over his lap, Wyld pointed to the cooked eggs. "Three eggs and as many pieces of bacon, Harry."

Beest complied then added a few pieces of toast and passed the plate back to Wyld. As he started filling his own, Louis reappeared with a second, smaller cart on which was a steel pot of coffee, three porcelain cups, a creamer and sugar bowl. He swiftly set these between the food trays. He then poured two full cups and set them before his diners.

"Will there be anything else, sir?"

"That will be all for now, Louis. Thank you."

Taking a careful sip of the hot brew, Beest waited until the portly cook was gone before continuing his earlier conversation.

"Something big in the wind, Mr. Wyld?"

"I'm not quite sure," Wyld replied, spooning sugar into his coffee. "Big Swede Jorgenson has been making some aggressive moves lately and I'm not convinced they are harmless to our own interests."

"You think he wants a bigger piece of the pie?"

"Of course he does. That's the nature of our business. No, it's just his timing that has me concerned. If he moves too fast he could start a whole new street war and that is something we can ill afford right now."

"What does Fat Jacob say?"

"Mr. Wiseman advised I take a wait and see attitude. He doesn't see Big Swede's activities as anything to worry about. Yet."

"So, what are you going to do?"

"I'm going to meet with Police Commissioner Henkle. Same old rendezvous location out on Sutter's Point."

Beest swallowed a tasty piece of bacon. "You think Henkle has some arrangement with Big Swede?"

"Aside from collecting his weekly paycheck, as he does from every other gang boss in the city, no, I don't. Rather, I want Henkle to alert his men to keep an eye on Swede's people over the next few weeks. See if they're involved with anything other than their normal activities."

"Sorta making the coppers your eyes and ears, eh, Mr. Wyld."

"Exactly. With all the money we've paid Henkle these past few years, it's time he started earning some of it."

Before Beest could add anything further, the hall door opened and Alexis Wyld walked in dressed in flats, white stockings, a plaid skirt and off-white blouse. Her long black hair cascaded down to her shoulders and bobbed back and forth as she moved.

"Alexis, good morning my dear," Topper Wyld greeted with a warm smile.

Surprised to see Harry Beest with her father, Alexis' own lovely smile faltered for a second, then she quickly replaced it. She walked over to her father and leaning down planted a kiss on his cheek.

"Good morning father." She looked back at the bodyguard. "Harry."

"Morning, Miss Wyld."

Alexis pulled out the chair to father's right and sat. Two seconds later Chef Louis' reappeared carrying a tray on which was a glass of orange juice; Alexis' usual morning drink.

"Good morning, Madam," he said, placing the tray before her. "Can I get you anything special?"

"Ooh, blueberry muffins," she squealed joyfully. "Just some warm butter, Louis."

"Coming right up." He bowed and vanished back into the kitchen wiping his hands on his apron.

"Will Miss Minault be joining us?" Wyld asked his daughter as he plucked a muffin off the tray and set it on her own empty plate.

"I don't know. She was still asleep when I went past her room."

"That's probably my fault," Beest said. "She asked me to take her downtown shopping last evening and we had dinner together at Red Rooster. Guess we had a little too much wine with our food. Anyway, she was pretty much wiped out by the time I got her back to her room."

Alexis Wyld couldn't believe how smoothly Harry Beest lied. Neither he or Yvette had been tipsy at all when they'd gotten home. What was he trying to pull? Meanwhile Beest took another sip of coffee and simply smiled at her.

"Well did you have a schedule planned for today's lessons?" Wyld posed, wiping his mouth with a napkin.

"She's teaching me world history and was hoping we could visit the Cultural Museum later today."

"Well, my dear, I'm sure Miss Minault won't be too late. She has proven to be a very conscientious young lady."

A ring sounded from the kitchen and then Louis appeared carrying a small tub of melted yellow butter.

"Telephone for you, Mr. Wyld," he announced placing the small bowl in front of Alexis.

"Thank you, Chef," Wyld pushed back his chair to rise. "You'll both excuse me."

"'Sokay, Boss," Beest set down his cup. "I need to go gas up the car. I'll be back in twenty minutes."

"That's fine, Harry, I'll be ready to go by then."

Chef Louis and Topper Wyld exited the room and Harry finished his coffee. He got to his feet and leaned over the table as Alexis was about to slather butter on her muffin.

"Little mice shouldn't go about hiding in people's closets," he chuckled.

"Wha—" Her mouth fell open at the realization he had knew of her presence the night before. "I don't know what you're talking about."

"Of course you do, little mouse." He turned and started for the door. As he began to push it open looked back over his shoulder and smile again. "Maybe you learned a thing or two for when you study all about the birds and the bees. Ha, ha, ha."

Alexis felt her cheeks redden as the door swung closed behind him. That man was insufferable. One day she'd teach him a lesson or two. It was a vow she was determined to keep.

CHAPTER (10)

Waldo Dunzinger waited until after ten p.m. before driving his beat-up panel truck through the side streets and alleys of Old Town by the docks. As the beams of his headlamps lanced across the junk-littered narrow roads, his eyes peered into the darkness searching for any homeless vagrants, hobos or bums that might prove to be a likely target. Weeks before it had been stray dogs he'd been searching for. This really wasn't much different. The natural stench of these forgotten lanes combined with the briny salt smell of the ocean made for a rich odor he was all too familiar with. At one time in his own past, the hideously deformed Waldo had been one of these lost denizens, with no roof over his head or food in his belly. Had it not been for his encounter with Professor Bugosi, he might still be among these throw away people forgotten by society.

Which was why, though he had his own misgivings about what he had been ordered to do, Waldo could not disobey the professor. He owed the man everything and so on this average midweek night, he quieted the voice of his nagging conscience. Bugosi wanted a man to experiment on and Waldo would get him one.

The air was chilly and he was glad he had worn his heavy gray wool jacket and newsboy cap. In the back were blankets and other assorted junk. All he could put to use if he found a likely candidate.

It didn't take him long. Turning into one side street situated between two massive warehouses, Waldo came upon a cluster of wooden pallets that had been assembled against one of the building's brick walls to create makeshift shelters for a half dozen men. Four of them were hunkered around an empty barrel in which a fire was blazing. He eased up on the gas pedal, came to a stop and shut off the engine.

Before exiting the cab, he picked up the bottle on the seat beside him and carefully made sure not to drop it as he stepped down to the pavement.

By now the quartet warming up at the drum was eyeing him warily and he suspected they were ready to run should he prove hostile. These were beaten men whose very survival depended on their not trusting anyone, ever. Two were white, one a Negro and other appeared Chinese.

"Who da hell are you?" A biggest of the whites queried menacingly. He wore a heavy black coat and an old captain's cap. He had an unshaven square jaw and towered over the three circling the high rising yellow flames. "And what d'ya want here?"

"My boss needs another man to work for him," Waldo answered, having concocted his story during his drive across town.

"Who your boss?" a little oriental wanted to know in pidgin English. When he turned to Waldo, the fire illuminated his round yellow face and the fact that his left eye had been replaced by a glass orb that eerily reflected the flames.

"He's a professor," Waldo said. "He owns a big house and needs someone to help me keep it clean and in good shape."

"Oh, yeah," the big guy spoke again. The other three seem to defer to him. It was obvious his size made him their natural leader. Dunzinger could appreciate that. "So what's he paying?"

"Three dollars a day and all the food you can eat."

"Really?" Waldo held up the bottle he was holding. "And a little nip every now and then, if your work is satisfactory."

At that the black man smiled showing off his rotting teeth and reached out to grab the booze offering. "Now you're talkin', pally."

"Hold up," Waldo pulled it away from the drunk's grasp. "This is only to seal a deal." He looked at all four men individually. "We got any takers here."

The shorter white dude, wearing a knit cap and ratty blue scarf, wiped the back of his hands over his puffy lips clearly imagining the taste of the alcohol. "I sure could use a drink, Lem."

"Yeah, we all could," the big man agreed, thus identifying himself as Lem. He walked around the others to face Waldo up close. "Okay, I could use the job. Give with the bottle."

Waldo handed it over and watched as Lem uncorked the top and then took a long swallow. When he was done he passed it over to black fellow. "Here, Carl, you share it fair and square."

"Okay, Lem," Carl nodded eagerly grabbing the bottle. "You gonna go with that ugly giant?"

"Sure, why the hell not. Can't be any worse than things are here." Lem laughed and looked back at Waldo. "Come on, I'm ready when you are."

Waldo merely nodded and started back to the truck. Lem followed. As he did so he pulled a jackknife from his jacket pocket.

"You try anything funny, and I'll cut you open like a big old tuna. That clear enough?"

Waldo merely looked at the open blade and shrugged. Then he pointed to the cab of the truck. "Get in. We got a long drive."

Once back on the road, Waldo steered through traffic leaving the seedy docks behind. So far all had gone well.

Now for the second part.

"So what's this professor like?" Lem asked, nervously making conversation. He never saw Waldo ball his right hand into a fist.

He never saw the fist strike out catching him on the side of the head with a loud smack. Lem's head rocked to the side and with a loud sigh his entire body seemed to deflate upon itself. He was out cold. Waldo took his eyes off the road for a second to be sure. Satisfied the man wouldn't give him any trouble, he returned his attention to the street ahead.

He should be back at the mansion long before poor old Lem came to. Long enough to carry him into the house and lock him up in the steel cage that was about to be his new home.

Thinking about that, Waldo's feelings of guilt surfaced again. Still, there was nothing to be done about it. The Professor was the boss and that was that.

There was no arguing that Big Swede Jorgenson's Gray Owl Casino was the swankiest night spot in all of Cape Noire. All one had to do is drive past the glitzy downtown establishment at night and be blinded by its dazzling neon sign hanging high above the front entrance. Here the rich and famous mingled with corrupt city politicians and various entertainment celebrities while they spend their money on games of chance; from roulette to poker. There was also the main room where a full-sized-band played 'til the wee hours of the morning, allowing rich men and their ladies to dance the night away.

Of all his operations, it was Big Swede's most profitable.

Standing across the four lane boulevard watching the rich folks coming and going, Jack and Tommy Bonello puffed on their cigarettes nervously deciding which of casino's exiting patrons would make their best victim. It was almost one in the morning and they were aware the joint closed at two, so their time to find a likely patsy and strike was ticking away. Never mind the temperature had gotten considerably colder in the past few hours. Both paced back and forth in front of a pharmacy locked up for the night.

"I told ya this was a dumb idea," Tommy pulled the half-finished butt out of his mouth and spit on the sidewalk. "The joint's probably half empty by now," he argued, pointing to the club across the street. Several couples had just emerged and were hailing city yellow cabs.

"Stop being such a negative Nellie," Jack Bonello chuckled, taking a drag from his own coffin nail. "You gotta have faith. Tommy."

"Ha, ha, faith. Since when did you become a holy Joe? We've been out here all night and all we've done is freeze our asses off."

There was a loud blaring of a car horn and the twins turned to see several cars slamming on their brakes in the middle of the street. The cause of this sudden halt to traffic was immediately apparent. A man decked out in a fancy topcoat and white silk scarf with a top hat leaning precariously on his head walking crookedly across the road, weaving about in a drunker stupor.

Jack's eyes lit up and he smiled at his brother. "Well lookee there, Tommy boy." He nodded towards the drunk heading in their direction. "Now that's what I call answered prayer."

He tossed away his cigarette and jogged out into the road waving his arms at the stopped cars and shouting, "Hold up! Hold up!"

Cabbies were yelling obscenities out their open windows while others made recognizable gestures with their fingers. Jack Bonello ignored them and finally reached the swaying fellow as he was about to fall over. Hurriedly he reached out and took hold of the guy's right shoulder and propped him up.

"Hey, hang on there. I got you."

"You do, heh," the drunk commented, his breath reeking of bourbon. Jack turned his face away from the smell as he began guiding the fellow to the sidewalk. Behind them cars once again began to roll past. After a few anxious minutes, he was at the sidewalk with Tommy grabbing the dude's left arm.

"That was nuts, Jack," his brother criticized. "You coulda' been hit the way those hacks drive around here."

"Ah, back off Tommy. We couldn't let our friend here get hurt could we?" Jack looked into the drunk's face.

The guy wasn't a bad looking swell and appeared to be in his late twenties, early thirties. His threads were quality, from the tuxedo itself to his shiny black shoes and wobbly top silk hat.

"What's your name, mister?" Jack asked, exuding friendly charm.

"Dan. But you can call me Danny," the tipsy fellow gave him a lopsided grin. "Say, why is the world spinning?"

Both Bonello brothers chuckled at that observation. Danny boy was totally out of it and wouldn't offer them any problems.

"So, where were you going...crossing the street like that?" Jack continued the conversation as he and Tommy continued to lead the man away from the street and towards the alley alongside the drugstore.

"My car's around here someplace," Dan the Drunk replied. He looked around, bewildered for a moment and wiped a hand over his eyes, blinking them several times. "I parked it down one of these side streets. Maybe this one right here." He pointed to the alleyway that was their destination.

"Then let us help you find it," Tommy spoke up for the first time. "It must be right back here somewhere."

"Yup. You boys are very good chaps."

Picking up their pace, the twin teenagers shuffled their rich target further into the shadows of the alley until there was barely enough light for any of them to see. In the back of the building was an empty lot filled with rubbish cans and dumpsters used by surrounding businesses. Among these rats scurried about doing their best to elude several mangy tomcats in search of a fresh meal.

"This is far enough," Jack declared and tightened his grip on the inebriated Mr. Dan.

"It is," he slurred his words, again looking around. "I don't see anything, boys."

"That's because there's nothing to see," Jack's tone became serious. "Now why don't you just give us your wallet and we'll let you sleep it off in one of those dumpsters."

"Huh...wallet?"

"You heard my brother," Tommy added reaching behind his back. Beneath his denim jacket he pulled out the police revolver and pointed it at their victim. "Give us your wallet now!"

"Hey, is that a real gun?" Mr. Dan shouted. "You got a gun. What are you, some kind of cowboy?"

"Shit, stop shouting, you fool," Jack warned. "Just give us your goddamn wallet."

"All right, all right," Dan Rains said, soberly assured that his voice had carried far enough for their trap to be set. Sure enough, a beam of light suddenly splashed across the darkened area as Officer Terrence Duseault appeared from behind them. Though his light played across Tommy's eyes blinding him, his words were loud and clear.

"Police, drop the gun kid, or I'll shoot."

Before Tommy could react, Rains pushed Jack away at the same time spinning around and snatching the revolver out of the kid's hand. "I'll take that."

"What the hell!" Tommy gasped throwing a hand up to shield his eyes.

Without waiting a second longer, Jack Bonello started running into the Stygian darkness.

Rains shoved the revolver in his pocket as he took off right behind him and before they'd gone a few yards, he jumped and tackled the fleeing mugger. They both slammed into several trash cans and rolled around in the muck. Rains' top hat went flying while rats sprang out of crevices to get out of their way. On his back, Jack Bonello tried to punch the cop.

"Enough!" Rains barked, as he rose up sitting on the youth and drove his right fist into his jaw. That took the fight out of the boy. "You two just don't know when to quit, do you?" He got to his feet and reaching down, took hold of Jack's jacket and pulled him up. The boy was holding his jaw trying to stay conscious.

"Asshole," he cursed groggily.

"Shut up," Detective Rains. "You and your brother are under arrest for the murder of Police Officer Milo Murphy." With Officer Duseault's flashlight on him, he looked around until he spotted the tall silk hat and picked it up. Only then did he see the tux was covered in dirt and torn in several spots. "Aw, damn it."

"Looks like you got your tux dirty," the copper said as he shoved Tommy Bonello towards the detective. He'd already put handcuffs on the boy. "Captain ain't gonna be happy about that. Rental store is going hit the department with the cleaning bill."

"Yeah, well at least it got us these two," Rains rebutted, as he pulled handcuffs from his other pocket and began to put them on Jack. "It's the results that count."

"If you say so," Duseault grinned. He looked at the twins and waved his pistol at them. "Let's go. We got a nice cell waiting for you boys at the precinct."

The four walked off leaving the lot to the vermin and the feral felines.

The sun was shining unusually bright over Cape Noire by the time Lt. Detective Clement Serat parked his old navy blue Pontiac behind precinct headquarters. Shutting off the engine, a glance at his Timex informed him that he was already twenty minutes late for his shift. At that, he looked at himself in his rearview mirror and smiled. That was one of the benefits of being plainclothes, the relaxed attitude that permeated the detective squad; unlike the uniformed boys who had to make roll call and put up with stiff-necked duty sergeants who were always finding things wrong with how they did their jobs.

No siree, those days were long behind him, he thought as he climbed out of the car, his sizeable gut making it more of a chore every day. Gloria had to stop feeding him so damn well. Every morning it was bacon and eggs, juice, and tall stack of pancakes with thick maple syrup. Just recalling it made him belch.

LT. DETECTIVE CLEMENT SERAT PARKED HIS OLD PONTIAC BEHIND THE PRECINCT.

Geez, maybe I should go on a diet. The thought stopped him half way to the building's back entrance. *Ha, who the hell am I kidding. Just gotta have to tell Gloria to stop fattening me up like a prized bull.*

The steel back door opened and he looked up to see his young protégé, Detective Dan Rains exiting. Rains saw him and his eyes lit up.

"Serat, great. I was worried I wouldn't see you before you came in." The rookie investigator said, jogging down the four concrete stairs.

"Well here I am," Serat declared jokingly. "What's new?"

"Duseault and I caught the Bonello brothers last night."

"What?" Serat was taken by surprise. "How? Where?"

"Outside the Gray Owl Club after midnight. I dressed up like a drunk playboy and they tried to jump me in the alley across the street." Rains was having trouble containing his enthusiasm. "It was classic decoy entrapment just like they taught us at the academy."

Serat tilted his fedora back on his head, trying to decide if what he'd been told was good news or bad. "Ah, right. Good work, kid. Where are they now?"

"In the holding cells. Assistant D.A. wants them before a judge by ten for arraignment. Oh, and that's the other good news."

"Oh, what's that?"

"They had Officer Murphy's gun on them. D.A. says with that as evidence, the case is going to be a sure thing."

"Yeah, I suppose so." Serat's thoughts were whirling around like a runaway circus carousel. "Well, I guess we're going to have celebrate later when you are off night duty."

"That'd be great. But right now all I want to do is get some breakfast, head home and get some sleep."

"I don't blame you." Serat reached and shook Rains' hand. "Good job, Rains. Now get the hell out of here."

"Right. See you later."

Clement Serat watched his young charge jog away down the busy street and then shook his head. Who'd have thought the kid could pull it off? But he had and now the veteran copper had another job to take care. He turned, walked up the stairs and entered the precinct.

The detective offices were on the second floor and he walked to them using the back wall staircase. Once in the open area where ten desks were aligned, five on each side of the long rectangular room, he was greeted by several of his colleagues already busy with their various cases. A few banged away on typewriters while others were gabbing away on their black phones. The shades along the front windows had all been pulled halfway down to block the searing white light from the shining sun.

Serat's desk was at the far end of the room away from the captain's office, which had always suited him fine. It was never a good thing to have the boss breathing down one's neck all the time. Serat took off his wrinkled brown suit coat and hung it on the clothes rack behind his desk and then placed his hat atop it.

He pulled back his wheeled chair, sad down and immediately unbuttoned his shirt sleeves and rolled them up. Then he took his black candlestick phone, tapped the hook and gave the switchboard operator the number he wanted. As she dialed, he cradled the receiver between his head and shoulder and pulled out his pack of Lucky Strikes from his left breast pocket. On the desk was a box of wooden matches snatching one he had his cigarette, the third of the day thus far, lit by the time his connection was made.

"The offices of Jacob Wiseman, Attorney at Law. How may I help you?"

"This is Ben Arnold, I need to speak with Mr. Wiseman immediately."

"Please hold a moment, Mr. Arnold."

Serat inhaled tobacco letting it soothe him. There was a second click on the line and then the voice of Fat Jacob was in his ear.

"Wiseman here. Who is this?"

"It's Serat at the precinct."

"Ah, Detective Serat. Ben Arnold as in Benedict Arnold. Amusing. What do you have for me?"

"You wanted to know if and when those two twins were picked up."

"The ones who killed the policeman, yes."

"Well, they're in lock up right now . And in about another two hours they'll be in the downtown courthouse."

"I see. Very well. I'll take it from here."

"Is there anything you need me to do?"

"Yes, simply sit tight and wait for further instructions. Good day, Mr. Arnold."

Then the line was dead.

Detective Serat sat back in his chair and exhaled gray smoke towards the ceiling. He began to imagine a very nice big paycheck. And not from the department.

CHAPTER (11)

Big Swede Jorgenson sat up in his luxurious bed, his back against the padded headboard, enjoying the sight of Betty One-Eye dressing. Even pushing sixty, Jorgenson was a physically fit man easily possessing the strength of men half his age. And still his statuesque redhead was more than his match when it came to satisfying their carnal appetites. Although he was very much her boss in all things outside of the bedroom, when the two of them stripped and tangled, he had no illusions as to who was really in command. The woman was insatiable and most nights it was he who had to eventually give in to exhaustion.

Damn, but she's an animal, he mused watching her lace up her heavy black boots. She'd donned her slacks and dark gray cotton shirt unbuttoned over her torso. She'd already braided her long hair into a pony tail and when putting on the shirt she had yanked it up behind her head and let it drop down her arms and onto her back. As she stood and began buttoning her shirt, Big Swede caught a quick glimpse of her melon sized breasts. She looked up and caught him grinning.

"You want I should come back to bed?" she smiled wickedly.

"As much as my imagination says yes, my body needs to recover, woman. I swear at times it's as if you'll you want to kill me with sex."

"Would that be such a bad way to go?" Betty joked as she finished fixing the last button and then tucked the tunic into her pants. She went over to the dressing table on the other side of the room where she had set her leather shoulder holster with its .45 automatic. She slid her left arm through the loop and then the right adjusting the strap under her breasts so that the gun was snuggled tightly under her left arm, the butt ready to grasp should she need it quickly.

That done, she then picked up the small stiletto blade in its black sheath and bending over slid it into the top of her right boot.

"Let's hope I never have to find out," Jorgenson answered. "For now, we need to talk about strengthening our numbers."

Betty One-Eye came over and stood looking down at the crime king. "You think that's necessary? We've already got thirty men on the payroll."

"Normally I'd say yes, but at the same time I'm wondering what Topper Wyld's reaction is going to be to the recent acquisitions we've made."

"Seriously? You're worried about that old man?"

"Don't ever underestimate him," Jorgenson's face hardened. "He didn't gobble up half of Cape Noire by being soft. Topper Wyld is a ruthless son-of-a-bitch and sooner or later he and I are going to have to find out who is the top dog."

"Okay," Betty relented, sitting down on the edge of the bed. "So me and the boys will see what kind of muscle is out there that we can round up on the cheap."

"Excellent. Be back here by one this afternoon. I want to discuss our next moves and what's worth pursuing and what needs to stay neutral."

Betty One-Eye leaned over bringing her full lips to his at the same time her right hand snaked over the sheet and grabbed Jorgenson's organ. He gave a grunt through their kiss and she felt a definitive hardening in her grasp.

"Damn it, Betty, you're a she-devil," he gasped as she released her hold on him.

"Never said I wasn't, Boss."

"Get the hell out of here, before I lose whatever senses I have left."

The sadistic female soldier got to her feet and headed for the door, her shapely rear end offering Big Swede one final look at what was his alone.

Damn it. She just may be the end of me after all.

Having immigrated to America when he was ten years old, Nils Jorgenson hated living in cities. He missed the open fields of his homeland back in Sweden; the farmland and rivers. Thus shortly after rising to prominence in the Cape Noire crime world, Big Swede bought an abandoned thirty acre cattle farm in the country south of the city. He had the main house torn down and a three story monstrosity erected in its place. He also converted the giant barn to the right rear of his country mansion into a both a car garage on the ground floor and a twenty man barracks on the top for his rotating army of goons that patrolled the land day and night.

As one of his chief lieutenants, it was part of Betty One-Eye's duties to oversee this crew and make sure everyone was trained and efficient in their respective assignments.

This morning, coming out of the side door, she was easing into a black overcoat and whistling a melody she'd heard on the radio recently.

Among the cars parked outside the open doors of the bright red barn was her yellow painted convertible roadster. Leaning against the passenger door munching on an apple was her Mongolian colleague, Bulok Que. It being a warm day, he'd collapsed the canvas top into the back trunk space.

"Morning, Miss Betty," he greeted her, around a bite. He always called her "Miss Betty" even though she'd tried to dissuade him many times. In the end she merely accepted secretly thinking it was smart of the big man. A merciless warrior from a savage land, Que knew how respect his superiors.

Betty fished into her pockets; found the car keys and tossed them to long-haired Mongol.

"Here, you drive."

He caught the keys and moved around the front of the car while tossing aside the apple core. "Where to?"

"First Little Jamaica so we can pick up Eli." She pulled open the passenger door and dropped in the thick padded seat. "Then we'll decide from there."

In the year 1873 several hurricanes ravaged the islands of the Caribbean. The worst devastation struck Jamaica destroying sixty percent of the towns and killing over three thousand people. When news reached the states, it spread across the land and finally reached the home of Mr. Antoine Levalle, then one of Cape Noire's most successful export merchants. His personal interest was due to the fact that Levalle, a Frenchmen, had been raised on the island and before leaving to find his fortune in America, he'd married an island beauty named Petaine. It was she who upon learning of the tragedy that had befallen her beautiful home insisted Levalle do something to help her people.

Never one to deny Petaine's wishes, the wealthy trader commissioned one of his largest ships to sail to Jamaica and there gather the remnants of two hundred families, all of whom had suffered terrible losses and hardships, and bring them back to Cape Noire.

Upon their arrival several months later, he had them settled in brand new tenement buildings he had constructed for them in the district located on 8th Street to west Poe St. on the north and the Avalon woods to the south. From that time forth the triangle became known as Little Jamaica.

Betty One-Eye always felt uncomfortable whenever she was in the dirty, squalid ghetto of Little Jamaica. As Bulok Que motored them through the tight, narrow streets, he maintained a turtle's pace as people, especially shoeless children, ran back and forth through the streets as if they were their own private playground paying absolutely no attention to the cars and buses racing by. Most people avoided the three block area even if it meant driving several extra miles around it to reach their destinations.

In fact the only public organizations that were visible daily were the red and white buses of the Cape Noire Transit Authority and the police black and white radio patrol cars.

Puffing on a just lit cigarillo, Betty One-Eye had her right arm atop the door doing her best not to breathe in the particular smell of the place. It being Saturday, a farmer's market had been set up dead center of the small park in the middle of the neighborhood. Her sensitive nose recognized not only raw fish, but raw meat and poultry along with an assorted variety of vegetables and flowers. It was enough to make her sick. Thus the cigarillo.

When they turned a corner and came upon a group of little girls jumping rope, Que stepped on the brake and they stopped dead. Betty glared with her single eye at the four girls, two jumping and the other two holding the rope. None of the four acted as if they were even there.

"Hit the damn horn," she snapped.

The Mongolian complied, but the loud hoot had no effect on the four girls, each a different brown hue with kinky black hair. They just continued to jump, giggle and laugh.

Grabbing the top of the windshield with her left hand, Betty rose up to her feet yelling. "Get the hell out of the road!"

That stopped the jumpers who all turned to see who it was that had shouted.

Betty One-Eye returned their stare, the cigarillo still in her mouth. She had no idea what she was going to do if the little brats didn't move.

"Now, now," a soft, clear and delicate voice spoke up. "There's no reason for anyone to be upset here."

A tall, regal-looking woman with smooth ebony skin emerged from behind a pottery booth and stepped out in front of the roadster. She wore a long, sleeveless green dress with matching heels and an off-white silk shawl draped around her shoulders. On each slender arm were several copper bracelets and around her neck was a silk choker with an ivory white cameo dangling over her throat.

Betty sensed an aura of power as she scrutinized this new player. The woman's face seemed to have been chiseled from black stone, with high cheekbones, slim lips, a classic nose and two almost catlike brown eyes under arched eyebrows that any runaway model would have sold her soul for. Lastly the woman's hair was midnight black and tumbled down around her face like a frame. When she looked up at Betty, a very mysterious smile appeared at the corners of her mouth, while her piercing eyes remained cold and unmoved.

Immediately upon seeing her, the little girls collected their ropes and ran off, disappearing in the maze of vendor's stalls. The striking intruder turned to Betty and clasped her hands together in front of her body.

"See how easily a little matter is resolved."

"So, who the hell are you?" Betty One-Eye asked coldly. She didn't like being upstaged by anyone.

"I am the Countess Selena."

"Countess? You some kind of royalty?"

"It is merely a title given to me by the kind people of this community." As she spoke, Countess Selena moved out of the roadster's path and approached Betty One-Eye. The redhead tossed her cigarillo away as she dropped back in her seat. Her right hand slid beneath her coat to hold the butt of her automatic.

"You need not fear me, Beatrice McCauley. I hurt no one."

"Huh?" Hearing her name, the female gangster's grip tightened on her pistol. "How the hell do you know my name?"

Countess Selena stood before her and again smiled coyly. "It is both my gift and my curse to—shall we say—know things."

At that moment Elijah Saint Jonah appeared from out of the now gathering crowd and stood behind the strange woman having heard her response to his boss.

"That's because she's a voodoo priestess," he told Betty One-Eye. "Nothing happens in Little Jamaica that Countess Selena doesn't know."

"Ah, Elijah, you continue to walk a dangerous path," the Countess rebutted. "Many are the nights your poor Mama has cried herself to sleep. She too knows one day you will come to a violent end."

"Maybe, but until then stay out of my business and leave my Mama out of this." Saint Jonah took hold of the roadster and jumped into the small rear seat.

"What about me?" Betty One-Eye taunted the ebony colored seer. "Any predictions for me?"

Countess Selena's gaze bore down into Betty's face and for a moment seemed frozen and then she lifted her head and took a deep breath. "A terror follows your shadow, woman of one-eye. Heed my words, beware the monkey man."

"*Monkey man!* What's that suppose to mean?"

"Aw, she's just wacko," Eli said, from the back seat. "Let's get out of here."

Betty One-Eye slapped Bulok Que on the arm and said, "You heard the man. Let's roll. We got things to do."

With that the driver took his foot off the brakes and gave the car some gas. As it rolled off, Betty One-Eye took one quick glance back over her shoulder. Countess Selena stood there watching the car roll away.

Beware the monkey man! Betty One-Eye shook her head and began to laugh. Eli was right. The woman was nuts.

And still she would not ever forget the look on her face when she said those ridiculous words.

CHAPTER (12)

Detective Clement Serat was wrapping up a detailed homicide report he hoped would be the last duty of his day shift when his desk phone rang.

Please not another squeal, he thought picking up the black phone and holding the receiver to his right ear. He was tired and just wanted to go home to a nice home cooked meal and a half dozen beers.

"Detective Serat, Homicide," he declared with lackluster enthusiasm.

"This is Jacob Wiseman." Serat straightened up in his chair instantly alert. "Listen carefully. You are to go to the Gridiron Saloon at nine o'clock this evening. Go to the booth furthest in rear. Someone will be waiting there with instructions."

"Okay. I know where the place is."

"Good, do not be late."

"I won't be."

Click! The line was dead again. Serat held it away from his ear and looked at it with a sour expression on his face. As he replaced it on the cradle, he started making up what kind excuse he would give Gloria for going out at that hour. It wouldn't be difficult at all to come up with one. Gloria had been a cop's wife long enough to know such unexpected excursions were all too commonplace.

It was just after eight p.m. when Professor Bugosi and his assistant, Waldo, entered the back room of his upstairs laboratory. There, at the scientist's directive, the giant aide had constructed a strong steel cage similar to those used in most big city zoos. Only now the single inhabitant of the barred enclosure was Lem, the big homeless derelict Waldo had kidnapped two nights earlier. He lay on the cage floor wearing only his torn pants. His shoes and socks had been removed along with his jacket and shirt.

Since Waldo had carried him into the room that first night, Bugosi had made sure to keep his human guinea pig sedated until which time he was ready to proceed with his test. Thus twice a day he would inject the comatose man with a cocktail that kept him unconscious. Having finished concocting the formula that had been his goal since his meeting with Topper Wyld, the Professor had stopped using the knock-out drug that morning and as he had calculated, his subject was now beginning to stir.

Lem groaned and his body shook slightly.

"Hurry," Bugosi ordered, holding up the syringe with his special stimulant. "Get that door open before he is fully roused."

Waldo fumbled with the key for a second, his big hands not used to holding small objects. Finally the tip slid into the keyhole and he gave it a twist. The lock sprang and he pulled back the barred portal.

Prof. Bugosi rushed past him and went to the waking figure. Lem, still on the floor face down, was slowly beginning to move his head. Bugosi came up behind him, quietly knelt behind the man's field of vision and without hesitation plunged the needle into his neck.

Lem cried out in surprise, his head jerking up. Bugosi pushed the plunger in and then jumped to his feet, the empty syringe still in his hands. From the floor, Len looked back over his shoulder at the white-coated scientist, his face a mask of confusion and fear.

"Who the hell are you? Where am I?"

As he started to turn and sit up, he clutched the top of his forehead as if still dizzy. Prof. Bugosi wasted no time getting out of the cage and Waldo immediately locked the door behind him.

"Hey!" Lem blurted, seeing Waldo for the first time. "I know you," he declared now getting to his feet still a bit wobbly. "You're bastard who picked me up on the docks!"

Lem looked around and realizing his predicament grabbed the bars of the door only to discover it wouldn't open. "Hey, let me out of here? What the hell is going on here?"

At which point Bugosi stepped out from behind Waldo and smiled. "What is going on, my fine fellow, is a scientific experiment in which you are about to play a vital role."

"Experiment? What kind of experiment?"

"One to see if science can successfully unlock the dark side of a man's nature. In this case yours. In other words we are going to free your inner beast."

Lem started to ask another question when his body suddenly stiffened. His arms clutched the bars and a groan escaped his lips.

"*Argh*," he gasped. "What did you do to me." He pushed away from the door and doubled over clutching his stomach. "It burns! Inside me…"

Lem looked up at his captors, his face contorted in a pain-induced grimace. "Make it stop!" he begged. He took several steps back and then collapsed to the floor still holding his middle. His screams grew louder and he began to roll around frantically. His body contorted into grotesque angles as a strange transformation began to occur. Black hair began to cover his arms and naked torso as if emerging out of his skin like weeds in a garden.

"Look at his feet!" Waldo pointed. "They're getting longer!"

Sure enough each foot seemed to extend further by at least five inches and the toes curled radically with their nails becoming claws.

"Is he gonna change like the dogs did?" Waldo asked, now in a whisper, as he couldn't pull his eyes away from the metamorphosis happening in the cage.

"Not a dog," Bugosi corrected as he looked at the time piece he'd removed from his lab coat. "Something much more powerful and dangerous, Waldo. Watch and see."

Within minutes the man called Lem's entire face was covered with the same fine hair that had sprouted over the rest of his body. His ears had grown to sharp pink points and his nose tip swelled. His eyes had turned a dull, ugly yellow and when he opened his mouth, his teeth had become razor sharp fangs; milky white drool dripping from lips. All of which transpired in only six minutes.

Seeing his tormentors, the newly created wolf-man sprung up and took hold of the bars at the same time growling ferociously. Both Waldo and the Professor stepped back.

Maddened at his inability to reach them, the hairy monster took hold of two bars and began to push them outward with considerable strength. There was a screeching nose as the steel in his grasp began to bend.

"He's gonna break out!" Waldo warned turning to his still calm master.

"Impossible, Waldo. That's reinforced titanium steel. There's no way he can escape."

As much as Waldo had always trusted the Professor's judgment, this time he wasn't totally convinced. Lem, or what had been Lem, was barking at them now, spittle flying from his mouth; his yellow eyes almost popping from their sockets. Waldo took another step back assuring he could reach the room's exit should the creature succeed in snapping the cage door open. As much as he was devoted to Bugosi, he wasn't about to become wolf food for anyone.

Just then the wolf-man's entire body stiffened and he stopped growling. A look of confusion appeared on his savage face. His hands fell away from the cold steel and he stumbled backwards unable to maintain his balance.

"What's happening?" Waldo asked.

"Quiet!" Bugosi retorted. His gaze taking in every motion of his new furry entity.

The wolf-man's mouth gaped and a spray of blood gushed out. He fell to his side, twisted for a few seconds and then was still. He lay there unmoving.

Cautiously Prof. Bugosi approached the cage door. Waldo remained where he was.

"Is he dead, sir?"

"It appears so." Bugosi turned to his nervous assistant. "Open the damn door. I need to examine it."

Hesitantly Waldo moved past the scientist and once again put the key into the lock's hole. He had to twist it harder, as whatever damage the wolf-man had caused in bending the bars had also affected the locking gears. After several minutes, he managed to spring the catch pin and pull the door open a few inches. There he stopped.

"Are you sure, Professor? What if he's still alive?"

Bugosi had pulled a stethoscope out of his coat pocket and simply ignored his aide. He walked up to the unmoving figure and cautiously tapped the outstretched left arm with his shoe. There was no reaction. He kicked it a little harder. Still no response.

He looked down at the wolf-man's face, his eyes now glassy staring off into nothingness, his lower jaw covered in wet blood. Fairly confident of the beast's harmlessness, the Professor went down on one knee beside the body, adjusted the stethoscope in his ears. Then, leaning forward, he placed it on the hairy chest. There was nothing to hear.

Removing the medical hearing device he stood up and sighed deeply disappointed.

"What happened?" Waldo asked standing by the open door.

"I won't know until I do an autopsy, but it seems the transformation was too severe for his nervous system and it caused a major coronary failure."

"You mean he had a heart attack?"

"Yes, Waldo. It exploded."

"Gee, I'm sorry Professor."

"My dear Waldo, this is merely a temporary set-back. After all the change did happen. Now I have to refine the formula to adjust it to the human nervous system. It will be a while before we can report any viable progress to our benefactor, Mr. Wyld."

Bugosi walked out of the cage and looked up at his faithful servant. "Meanwhile get the remains on the operating table in the lab. Then tomorrow night you can go out and find us another subject."

Waldo watched his employer exit the room and then looked down at the dead wolf-man muttering under his breath, "Shit."

A light rain had started to fall on the city by the time Detective Serat entered the Gridiron Saloon. It was five minutes before nine, the appointed hour, and he marched directly towards the back of the rectangular barroom. At the bar, Ma McCoy and some guy Serat had never seen before, were busy pouring drinks to the loud and boisterous patrons on their stools.

He passed Peggy McCoy balancing a tray of empty bottles and mugs on his way.

"Bring me a draft," he told her pointing to the rear by the restrooms. "I'll be back there."

"Sure thing," she acknowledge without looking back.

Serat reached the last booth and there sat a very familiar figure. It was none other than Topper Wyld's rat-faced little weasel, Reed Vengel; better known as Revenge El. The corrupt cop disliked the crook but kept his feelings to himself. It wouldn't do any good to antagonize Vengel.

"About time you got here," Vengel said, as he lit up a cigarette and tossed the match into the glass ashtray by his half empty glass of beer.

"I'm on time," Serat countered sliding into the seat across from the small hood. "So what's this about?"

"Hold on," Vengel blew out a puff of smoke just as the waitress appeared and placed a fresh brew in front of Serat.

"Here you go."

"Put it on my tab," Vengel told her and she nodded before vanishing again.

Serat picked up his beer and held it up to Vengel. "Thanks." He took a drink and set it down carefully. "Again, why am I here?"

"Mr. Wyld needs you to do a job for him," Vengel grinned.

"What kind of job?"

"You got two young punks in lock-up for bumping off that bastard Milo Murphy."

"Yeah, one of the new guys on the force caught them and the idiots had Murphy's gun in their possession. D.A. is whistling Dixie now and says he's going to nail them both for murder one at their arraignments."

"Which is when exactly?"

"In two days."

Vengel exhaled a puff of nicotine smoke and then pulled a white envelope from his inner coat pocket. He dropped it front of Serat. The detective picked it up slowly and saw it was stuffed with hundred dollar bills.

"That's all yours, Serat. Spend it as you see fit to get the job done."

"Which is exactly what?"

"Make that gun disappear before those punks stand before the judge." Vengel smiled, his rat-like pointed nose and baddy eyes disgusting the dirty cop.

Serat took the envelope and carefully stuff it into his own jacket.

"Tell Wyld to consider it done."

CHAPTER (13)

Two days later Jack and Tommy Bonello were led into courtroom number three on the second floor of the Federal Building by two surly jail guards. Each of the boys was handcuffed and displayed several black and blue bruises on their faces; the results of their unwillingness to comply with jailhouse rules.

Sgt. Jake Welding was the senior guard and he directed the two boys to sit down behind one of the long wooden tables that faced the judge's bench; a five foot partition atop which the presiding official sat. Across the aisle from them was a second table and here several men in fancy suits were idly discussing other matters. One of them was Assistant District Attorney Owen Campbell. On the table before them were several briefcases and open folders.

Welding's partner, Guard Barney Lane took a seat behind the boys.

Neither of the twins had ever been in a courtroom before and they were a bit awed by the austerity of the open room, all the gallery seats behind them, and the American flag hung from a pole to the right of the bench. There also was also another slightly raised platform where there were thirteen chairs behind a short banister.

"Is that where the jury sits?" Tommy asked Jack.

Welding, sitting to Tommy's right, slapped the boy's arm hard. "Shut up and keep quiet. Any guff from either of you and I'll beat the crap out of both of you later."

Tommy's face turned red and he was just about to react when the door behind the bench opened and an old, gray-haired cop appeared followed by a man wearing a long black robe and carrying a folder in his hands.

"All rise in the court," the aged bailiff called out. "The honorable Judge Robert Ingram presiding." He then went and stood next to the wall, hands clasped behind his back.

Welding jumped to his feet and the boys followed his example, as did the men at the other table.

Judge Ingram was a man of average stature with a balding dome and tufts of white hair sprouting around each of his ears. He wore wire-rim glasses barely perched at the tip of his nose. He adjusted them a bit and looked at those standing before him. He turned to the prosecutor's table first.

"Good morning, Mr. Campbell. To what do we owe the pleasure of your presence today?"

ADA Campbell straightened the lapels of his charcoal gray suit before replying. "What we believe will be a very open and shut case, Your Honor." He smiled confidently.

"Well, that remains to be seen doesn't it?" Ingram then looked at the Bonello brothers and opened his folder to read the charges listed there.

"Tommy Bonello and Jack Bonello. That would be the two of you?"

"Yeah, that's us," Jack said. "We was railroaded by the damn..."

Welding cuffed the lad across the back of the head. "Shut up and just answer the questions."

"Hmm, that won't be necessary, Sgt. Welding. I'm sure once these young men comprehend the gravity of their situation, things will proceed smoothly."

"Yes, your honor." Welding was clearly anticipating the beating he would dispense on the punks when they were back at city lock-up.

"Now boys, this is an arraignment. Do either of you know what that means?"

Jack and Tommy looked at each other in bewilderment and then back at the judge. Tommy answered, "Ah, no, we don't."

"You are here to hear the charges the state has filed against you and then to give the court your plea." Ingram looked down at the record again. "You are simultaneously charged with three counts of aggravated assault and the first degree murder of a police officer, one Officer Milo Murphy."

"That's a lie!" Jack retorted, then flinched when Welding started to raise his fist again.

Judge Ingram grabbed a small wooden gavel and banged it hard before pointing it at the brothers. "I'll have no more such outbursts, young man. Is that understood?"

"Yeah," Jack hung his head in defeat.

"Were you boys apprised of your rights to an attorney?"

Tommy answered. "Somebody said something about that but we didn't understand what it meant."

"It means you need a lawyer, young man. And if you don't have one, then the court will appoint a public defender to represent you."

At which point the main doors to the room were pulled opened and in walked Fat Jacob Wiseman. "That will not be necessary, Your Honor." He marched his obese round body down the aisle like a conquering general in a tailor-made, three-piece-suit, a boutonniere in his lapel and his rich leather briefcase swinging from his left hand. "If it pleases the court, I would like to offer my services to these poor, misguided lads."

"Mr. Wiseman, what a wonderful surprise." Ingram's voice was laced with sarcasm.

"Why thank you, Your Honor." Wiseman waved his hand at Welding indicating he should step away. The guard looked up at the judge in momentary confusion and then joined his partner in the first row of the gallery seats. "If I may have a moment to confer with my clients?"

"Yes, but please hurry it up. We haven't got all day."

Wiseman could see the brothers were confused and he motioned them to approach him in a tight huddle which he could whisper his intentions. "I have been hired by someone who wants help you beat these charges. But

I can only do that if you agree to do exactly what I say.

"Is it a deal?"

"Don't see where we got any other choice," Jack capitulated. "Okay, pal, whatever you say goes."

"Excellent."

Attorney Wiseman turned to the judge. "My clients are ready to proceed, Your Honor."

Judge Ingram nodded. "Very well. Having read the charges, how do you plead? I need an answer from both of you."

Wiseman again whispered instructions to the twins.

"Not guilty," Jack Bonello spoke up.

"Not guilty," Tommy echoed.

Ingram tugged his chin with his left hand, the right still gripping the gavel. "Very well, if that is your decision, we'll set a date for your hearing."

"Your honor," Wiseman raised his hand. "At this time, I'd like to move to have the murder charge dismissed."

"On what grounds, counselor?"

"On the grounds that the state has insufficient evidence to warrant the charge."

"What!" ADA Campbell jumped to his feet. "I object, Your Honor. The state has in its possession hard evidence that will prove one of the brothers shot Officer Murphy with his own weapon and both were later apprehended with it in their possession."

"I see." Ingram slapped the gavel. "Motion denied."

Smiling at his victory, Campbell decided to press on. "The state also request bail be denied due to the severity of the crime."

"Your Honor," Wiseman had expected the move. "I respectfully would point out this is the first time my clients have ever been arrested and I am willing to accept full responsibility for them if the court will remand them to my custody until the time of their trial."

Once again the judge looked from bench to bench mulling over his decision. It only took him a few minutes.

"Very well, Mr. Wiseman. Bail is set at five thousand dollars. Are you willing to meet that amount?"

Wiseman never blinked. "I am, Your Honor."

Once again the gavel fell. "Then this hearing is concluded, gentlemen, with the defendants remanded to the care of Mr. Wiseman until the date of their court appearance. My clerk will inform both of you of the official date of the trial. Good day, gentlemen."

"VERY WELL, MR. WISEMAN. BAIL IS SET AT FIVE THOUSAND DOLLARS."

As Ingram stood, the bailiff once again commanded all to stand. Once he was gone, Wiseman turned to the guards and pointed to the handcuffs still on the boys' wrists. As Welding began to undo them, ADA Campbell approached the fat lawyer.

"What's going on here, Wiseman?"

"Why the pursuit of justice, of course."

"Don't give me that guff. What's Topper Wyld's involvement in this? What does he care what happens to two street punks like them?"

"I assure you, Mr. Campbell, that is none of my concern. I am merely providing the lads with representation, which is their right under law."

Seeing that Welding had taken off both sets of steel bracelets, Wiseman began ushering the Bonello twins to the exit door.

Campbell watched them leave and felt his stomach going sour. He went back to his table where his assistant, Lou Nolan, was closing up their briefcase.

"I don't like this, Lou. Something stinks if Topper Wyld is involved."

"How do you mean, sir?"

"Soon as we get back to the office, call the precinct and have that detective Rains check to see if the gun is still secured in the evidence room."

"You think someone may have tampered with it?"

To that, ADA Campbell didn't have an answer.

Detective Clement Serat was walking through the basement hall of the precinct when he heard someone shouting. He and several uniformed officers also in the corridor stopped and looked to where the voice was originating. It was the evidence room at the end of the hall.

Serat changed direction and headed for the cavernous room where all physical evidence was tagged and stored. He pushed opened the door to find his new protégé, Detective Dan Rains standing by the desk partition haranguing Police Clerk Davy Penz.

"Well look again!" Rains ordered, his face starting to turn red.

"Whoa, what's going on here?" Serat held up his hands palms out.

Rains took a deep breath and replied, "This idiot lost Murphy's gun."

"What?"

"The Assistant D.A. just called," Rains elaborated. "Told me to come and check to make sure the gun was safely locked up down here. It's his one piece of solid evidence to convict those Bonello boys.

"So I come down here, hand Penz my ticket-tag and he goes out back," Rains pointed to the long rows of steel shelves behind the clerk's desk, "only to have him come back ten minutes later with an empty box."

At this juncture, the shaken Penz, a small fellow with glasses and thinning brown hair, held up the cardboard evidence container on which was stenciled the numbers 1-4-8-7. Also in his fingers was a paper ticket with the identical same numbers.

"It's gone, Lieutenant," Penz pleaded. "I know I put it in this box two days ago. But now it's just gone."

"Well, did anyone check it out between then and now?" Serat referred to the open log register atop Penz's desk. Anyone picking up or depositing an item had to sign their names on the register, number of the item and the date and hour.

"No one, Lieutenant. I swear. The only entry is when Detective Rains here brought it in two days ago."

Serat did his best to look serious, all the while he knew exactly what had happened to Officer Murphy's weapon. He himself had gotten into the evidence room the night before using a skeleton key and snatched the gun. Now it was at the bottom of the harbor where no one would ever find it.

"What the hell are we supposed to do now?" Rains queried, his face a mask of sheer frustration.

"Well, maybe Davy put it in the wrong box. We're going to go back there and give him a hand making sure that didn't happen. If that isn't the case, then we're going to have to notify the Captain and the shit's gonna hit the fan big time."

Penz and Rains merely nodded.

"And then, Danny boy, you're going to call the D.A. and give him the bad news."

CHAPTER (14)

The long black hearse pulled up to the elegant mansion and came to an easy stop. The chauffeur jumped out and hurried to open the back door. Fat Jacob Wiseman emerged followed by the Bonello twins. Once out of the car, the boys stood side by side looking up at the impressive building and wondered why they had been brought there.

"I suggest you both be on your best behavior," the obese attorney advised as he started up the four steps to the front door. "Mr. Wyld does not appreciate impolite children."

Before either Jack or Tommy could offer up a caustic reply, the big door opened and out stepped Harry Beest wearing a dark blue suit, white shirt and light gray tie. His handsome face was devoid of expression as he eyed the two boys all but hid behind the rotund lawyer.

"Good day, Mr. Wiseman," Beest merely nodded.

"Harry. I take it Mr. Wyld is in his office."

"He is. Go on in and leave these two with me." Beest indicated the two brothers. "The Boss wants to talk to you before he sees them."

"Understood." Wiseman turned to the twins. "Stay with Mr. Beest here and behave."

He walked into the foyer and made for the hall that led to Topper Wyld's private office. After the boys had entered, Beest closed the door behind them and pointed to a large den to their right. "In there."

The boys complied, all the while their heads kept swiveling back and forth as they took in the opulent decorations and expensive furnishings. At the same time Beest studied them carefully. It was eerie just how much they looked alike, resembling mirror images of each other. They also moved in the same lithe manner reminding him of feral cats on the prowl. There was an animal quality about the brothers that he suspected hid brutal basic instincts. Instincts that depended on unleashed violence to survive.

Sure hope the Boss knows what he's doing.

Jacob Wiseman found Topper Wyld going over accounting books seated behind his desk. His briarwood pipe in his mouth, a sweet cherry blend smoke perfumed the office.

Topper pointed to the liquor drawer and invited his visitor to pour them each a brandy.

"So what do you have for me, Jacob?" Wyld asked as he closed the ledger he'd been reading and sat back in his padded chair. "Just who are these street urchins you've delivered to my doorstep."

"Well, I can tell they aren't Romulus and Remus about to establish Rome," the lawyer replied, filling two snifters with the ruby-colored liquor. He then handed Wyld a glass before dropping carefully onto one of the two straight-back chairs facing the desk.

"Understood." Wyld took a sip of his sweet drink. "How much of their history have you been able to learn?"

Wiseman smacked his lips enjoying the taste of the expensive brandy and then launched into his report. "Jack and Tommy Bonello were the children of an unwed prostitute working in Old Town. Addicted to drugs, she died of an overdose when the boys were seven, whereupon they were shipped off to the Ridgeway Orphanage up on Castle Harbor.

"The place is a shit-hole and from what I've been able to learn from one of the teachers still there, the boys gave the staff trouble from day one. Most of the time they were in detention for one violation or another. But no matter how severe their punishments, they never relented."

"Sounds like a pair of hardcases," Wyld commented.

"Indeed, an apt description."

"Go on, Jacob. What transpired next."

"They lasted in Ridgeway for two years before running away and coming back to Cape Noire. Keep in mind they were only nine by then. And somehow they've managed to survive the last six years on these streets on their own. Without a home, adult supervision or any such comfort most of us take for granted daily."

"So how did they live?"

"By stealing whatever they needed from day to day. Pretty soon they became well known in the neighborhoods around the docks and most people simply avoided them as best they could."

Wyld finished his brandy and puffed on his pipe for a few seconds. "And in all that time they were never picked up by the cops?"

"No sir. They obviously have an uncanny talent for disappearing when the police were looking for them. Which, from what I've gathered, was a weekly affair. As they made their home in those myriad back alleys and side streets, it's easy to see how they could elude the law and rival gangs for so long."

"Until now."

"Until now. Apparently this Officer Murphy was a bully with a badge and had been chasing the boys for quite some time, boasting he would see them locked up if it was the last thing he ever did."

"Apparently he got that part correct," Wyld said wryly, blowing out a wispy cloud of smoke. "So did they actually kill him?"

"It would appear so. From the police report, it seems Murphy caught the boys in an alley and attempted to beat them fiercely, only to have the two of them overwhelm him, grab his pistol and shoot him in the head with it.

"They had the weapon on them when they were finally apprehended."

"Hmm, seems like an open and shut case for the District Attorney."

"It was," Wiseman nodded, a smile on his round face. "Until that piece of evidence mysteriously vanished and is now where they will never find it. Thanks to one of our people in the precinct."

"Good work, Jacob. So where do they stand with the other charges filed them against them?"

"They are all minor charges for petty crimes. And considering I can argue this is their first offense, I'm sure Judge Ingram will let them off with a few hours of community service and a slap on the hand."

"I'm sure he won't mind our generous contributions to his re-election campaign as well," Topper Wyld chuckled.

"There is one matter that still needs to be resolved, Mr. Wyld."

"And that is?"

"The boys are still minors and I doubt seriously I can get them released without establishing an adult guardian."

Topper Wyld blew out a few more tobacco mini-clouds as his eyes looked upward. Wiseman knew his employer was considering their options and wondered what his final decision would be. He did not have long to wait.

Wyld removed his pipe and looking at Wiseman intently, made known his wishes. "All right, I'll take on that role. You file whatever legal papers are required and have them ready for their next hearing. Declare them my wards."

Not many things surprised Fat Jacob Wiseman, but this request did. Wyld saw the look on his attorney's face and grinned.

"What is it Jacob? You don't think I'll make a good father to these rascals."

"I'm just surprised, sir, as to why you'd want to take on what is pretty much a double headache considering their past behavior."

"And that's where you don't see the big picture, my friend." Wyld slapped his hand on his desk. "If everything you've told me is true, these young boys are exactly the kind of men I can shape into loyal soldiers. With the help of Harry Beest, we can mold them into the killers nature intended them to be.

"Killers totally devoted to me and me alone. Now, Jacob, you tell me where else I can find men like that?"

Wiseman understood the logic of what Wyld intended, though he didn't know if he could pull it off or not.

"It's your call, Mr. Wyld. Just don't say I didn't warn you."

"Ha, point taken. Now I think we're finished here Jacob. Report to me when the court date has been set. On your way out, have Harry bring them in. It's time I met my new sons."

"Yes, sir." Wiseman rose with some difficulty, put down his empty snifter and exited the room. His job for the time being was finished.

The two boys who entered Topper Wyld's office five minutes later were what he'd expected to see. They were tall for their age, both coming up to Harry Beest's broad shoulders. But they were also emaciated and gaunt, their filthy clothes barely hanging on them; from their mud-caked shoes to their torn pants and dirty ripped shirts. Wyld wondered when was the last time they had eaten a real meal and not stolen scraps from various eateries and outdoor food markets.

Still, despite their mangy street-urchin attire, they were not bad looking young men and it was odd looking the exact same hairless handsome features on two different bodies. Those faces, though smeared and scratched up, were strong; each defined by piercing dark brown eyes and scraggly, unwashed black hair that was overly long down their necks.

"Meet Jack," Beest said, coming in behind them. He patted the boy to his right on the back and then reached out to the one on his left. "And Tommy Bonello."

"I'm Jack, you big gorilla," the second twin snapped.

Beest slapped him across the side of the head. "Shut your yap. I don't give a shit which one you are."

Wyld sat quietly smoking his pipe; amused by the boy's cockiness. Finally he took the briar and turned it upside down over a small tin can on his desk blotter. With his palm he tapped out the ashes. This done, he rose to his feet and walked around the desk and approached the two juvenile killers.

"Do you boys know who I am?" he asked casually.

"Yeah," the one to his left answered. "I seen pictures of you in the papers. You're Topper Wyld, the big boss."

"Good. Do you know why I've had you brought here?"

At that the brothers looked at each other, mutual puzzlement was etched on their faces. Then one of them shrugged. "Maybe you like boys instead of dames."

Beest started to bring his hand up again, but Wyld laughingly waved him off.

"Ha, I will say this for you boys, you got moxie. And I like moxie, especially in those who work for me.

"Would you boys like to work for me?"

"Huh?" Again confusion masked their faces. "Are you serious?" queried the one to his right.

"I am," Wyld clasped his hands together. "I am always on the lookout for good men who know how to take care of themselves. And from what I hear, you two are experts at that. You're tough and you don't back down. That's the kind of soldiers I want in my army."

"So, what's in it for us," Jack retorted. Or at least Wyld thought he was Jack.

"Well, for one thing, I'm going to make the murder charge against you boys go away and see you don't spend another single day behind bars."

"You can do that?"

"That and a whole lot more." Wyld was warming up. "If the two of you agree, you'll never go hungry again or be without a roof over your heads. If you join my little empire, men like Mr. Beest here will see that you are properly trained in all kinds of things you have never imagined. When he's done, you'll both be two of my top lieutenants and you'll have more money than you know what to do with."

"That sounds pretty good," Tommy admitted. "But how do we know it's legit. I mean you could just be conning us."

"It's no con. In fact, if you do agree, then I am going to become your legal guardian."

"What's that mean?" Tommy scratched the back of his ear.

"It means as far as the law is concerned, you two will be my wards. My sons."

"I don't get it," Jack repeated. "Again, why us?"

Wyld turned from the boys and walked over to the far wall to the right of his desk. There hung a framed topographical map of the Cape Noire. He pointed to it and looked back at them over his shoulder.

"Right now I own maybe thirty percent of this city, boys. But that's not enough. I want to own it all. That means in the years ahead, I'm going to have to fight other people to get it. To do that I will need loyal soldiers.

And I think the two of you can be that for me."

He turned around to face them directly. "So, what do you say? Yes, and your future is set. No and you can go back to jail. It's your call."

"All right," Jack Bonello said. His brother Tommy nodded his head in agreement.

"Excellent." Topper Wyld clapped his hands together and joined them. This time he addressed himself to Harry Beest. "Find rooms for them in the guest house on the same floor as your own. Get them washed up and then take them into town and buy them new clothes. Can't have my men looking like bums. After that take them to Sal's Spaghetti House and feed them properly."

"You got it, Boss."

As Beest started to usher them out of the office, Jack stopped and nervously looked back at Topper Wyld. "Er...thanks, Mr. Wyld."

Wyld smiled knowingly. "From now you can call me Boss."

Having taken the boys out the back door, Harry Beest began leading them to the large two story house behind the mansion. In front of the house, several tough looking men were gathered. They were all armed with shotguns. Upon seeing Harry, several called out hellos.

"This is where I and a few others live," he informed his charges. "There's always three men on duty all the time protecting Mr. Wyld and his daughter Alexis."

"Pretty fancy," Tommy approved. "How long you been working for him?"

"Ten years now. He's a hard man, Jack, but fair. Do what he says and both of you will do all right here."

"I'm Tommy," the boy declared.

"Shit," Beest cursed. "I ain't about to spend my time figuring out which of you is which. After we finish up at the spaghetti place, I'm taking you two to one more place."

"Yeah, where's that?"

"A tattoo parlor. Before this day is over, everyone is going to know who's Jack and who's Tommy."

CHAPTER (15)

Butch came down the back stairs to the Gridiron Saloon with a silly grin plastered over his face. From the moment he'd gotten out of bed an hour earlier, all he could think about was the previous night and his date with Peggy McCoy.

After months of working together side by side in the bar, and under her mother's constant prompting comments, he had finally gotten up the courage to ask her out. When he'd arrived at their apartment door, down the hall from his own, it was Molly who had yanked back the door and given him the once over.

"You clean up nice," she finally said, with a smirk. At which point Peggy had appeared from her bedroom in a beige floral dress he'd never seen before, high heel shoes, and a delicate cotton shawl draped over her shoulders. Her hair was tied up in a bun and he noticed immediately she had put on lipstick, though a very subtle pink.

"Mom, leave him alone," she chided gently pushing her mother aside. "Don't pay her no mind," she told him. "Oh, I know her all too well by now," he chuckled. "Let's get out of here before she says she wants to come along." At that all three of them laughed.

Once on the landing to the back stairs, Butch touched Peggy's arm and said, "You look lovely."

The compliment brought a blush to her cheeks and she didn't know what to say. Instead she took his hand in hers and that started down the stairs. Both of them hoping it was the start of a magical night.

It had been that and more.

Entering the bar, he all but danced his way to the kitchen while whistling. As usual Molly was already there putting away boxes of napkins in the pantry next to the sink. He sometimes wondered if she ever slept.

Hearing his whistling, she turned to greet him with her typical caustic humor. "Ah, Romeo appears at last. I was beginning wonder if you'd sleep all day."

"Ha, no way," he went to the counter, pulled open the drawer and withdrew a new apron which he tied about his middle. "It's too beautiful a day."

"That it is, my boy. That it is. Now I'll be needing you to go down into the cellar and carry up two new kegs. The ones under the bar are almost empty."

"Will do," he said, moving to basement door across from the pantry.

"Ah, did Peggy say anything about last night after she got home?"

"My, but ain't you the nosey one. And what makes you think I would have been up when the two of you two lovebirds came home?"

"I've got it on good authority that you never sleep, you old witch."

"Be off with you, smart mouth and get those kegs. What me daughter said was for me ears only. Understood. My lips are forever sealed."

Butch flicked on the light switch at the top of the wooden stairs and carefully made his way into the cellar. It was a small square cavern with a dirt floor on which wooden palettes had been set as a make-shift floor. Atop these were stacked boxes and a dozen shiny steel beer barrels. Butch went over to the nearest, bend down and heaved it up onto his right shoulder. Then carefully balancing it, he grabbed the railing and started back up the stairs.

He was half-way when he heard Molly moan followed by a loud crash. He forgot his hesitation and charged up the remaining stairs into the kitchen.

Molly McCoy was laying on her right side on the floor, her right arm extended above her head. She appeared unconscious.

"MOLLY!"

Butch set down the keg and rushed to her. On both knees beside her, he gently took hold of her shoulder and carefully maneuvered her onto her back.

"Molly! What's wrong?"

When she didn't answer, he leaned down with his ear next to her lips and was relieved to hear her breaths, shallow as they were. He took hold of her right hand and held it for a second.

He heard footsteps and looked back just a Peggy appeared. Seeing her mother on the floor, her eyes doubled in fear. "Mother!"

She knelt beside Butch. "What happened?"

"I don't know. I was downstairs getting a keg of beer when I heard her fall."

"What's wrong with her?"

"I don't know. Look, don't move her. But get a blanket and keep her warm."

Peggy was staring at her sleeping mother as if paralyzed. Butch shook her arm. "Did you hear me?"

She looked at him and blinked. "Yes, keep her warm you said."

"Good." He got to his feet. "I'm going to call an ambulance."

Running out of the kitchen, Butch Hammer began praying liked he'd never prayed before.

CHAPTER (16)

It was shortly after dinner and Prof. Bugosi was seated in his den enjoying his after meal brandy when his aid came through the door hurriedly.

"The truck from the circus has arrived," the hulking Waldo Dunzinger announced

"Excellent." Bugosi finished his drink, set the glass down and rose from his padded chair. "Where are they?"

"I told the driver to go around to the back entrance as you directed, sir."

Bugosi rubbed his hands together and started for the hall. "Well don't just stand there, Waldo. Let's go and meet them. The sooner we get the creature up to the lab the better I'll feel."

Waldo had all he could do to keep up with his eager employer.

The sun had set less than an hour earlier over the Pacific and its last rays clawed across the overhead sky like purple fingers. Soon the blue of the horizon would give way to blackness. As they exited the back door to the wooden porch, the big box truck was turning the corner to their left, its headlights not yet on. As Bugosi watched it drive up and then turn from the house itself and to aim at the surrounding woods, he observed the garish paintings that covered the vehicle with images of clowns and exotic animals such as elephants and tigers. Across this collage was a painted orange and white banner proclaiming Hatfield's Show of Wonders.

The driver tapped the brakes, and his passenger jumped out. He was a big man, wearing a leather jacket, work boots and a newsboy cap. He raced to the porch, acknowledged the Professor and Waldo with a quick nod and then, lining up with the rear of the lumbering truck, began to guide it backward towards the porch.

With his assistance, the driver skillfully backed up the heavy vehicle to the landing and brought it to a dead stop a mere few inches from making hard contact. The man then raced up the stairs to meet the scientist and his aide.

"Are you Bugosi?" he inquired, peeling a glove off his right hand.

"I am, sir. And you are...?"

"Paul Nary, Mr. Hatfield's chief roustabout." He extended his calloused hand. Bugosi shook it formally.

"And you have the animal?"

"As promised. Though I can't say Korgo appreciated the trip."

The Professor reached into his dinner jacket pocket and pulled out an envelope stuffed with cash. He handed it to the Nary. "Six thousand dollars as agreed upon."

"Thanks, Professor." Nary stuffed the payment into the back pocket of jeans. "Now, where do you want me and Jake to take Korgo?"

As they were conversing, the truck's driver, Jake—another big fellow wearing a chewed up fishing cap with a long bill—had joined them on the porch and was unlatching the truck's rear doors. Once done he easily pulled both panels aside so that what remained of twilight spilled into the darkened interior where they all could see the massive, furry thing chained to the floor and walls.

Korgo was a big silverback gorilla and it looked dazed and confused. Its legs were manacled to the truck's floor, while chains were wrapped around its powerful arms. Obviously male, its size and shape indicative of a fully grown behemoth well in excess of four hundreds. Its hands were huge, its gray hairless torso was massive. Pearl-like eyes were glazed in its black, rough-textured face.

"He looks ill," Bugosi observed.

"It's just the drugs we gave him," Nary explained pointing to a bunch of half-eaten bananas next to the gorilla's feet. "That's how we were able to get him on the truck and here without him ripping it to shreds. We doused his fruit with animal sedatives."

Bugosi understood. "How long will they last?"

By now Jake had entered the truck and took hold of a two-foot long cattle prod affixed to a hook mounted on the interior wall. He switched on the handle battery and tapped the duel electrodes at the end against the floor. Immediately sparks snapped from its tip. The high voltage shock the rod provided was enough to keep the massive Korgo in line should the animal become violent.

"Not much longer," the carny foreman cautioned, looking at his wrist-watch. "Which is why we need to get him to wherever you have your cage set up."

"That would be on the second floor in a room behind my lab."

"Upstairs?" Nary looked worried.

"The elevator is just inside this back door and my aide, Waldo here, will assist you gentlemen."

"All right, but let's make it fast. I don't want to deal with Korgo when awakens. He's already killed two of our people at the circus and maimed another."

"Then by all means, gentlemen, proceed." Bugosi took a step back and tapped Waldo on the arm. "Help them, Waldo, I'll go upstairs and get the cage ready for our new guest."

With a wicked smile, the delighted scientist disappeared back into the house.

"He wants to do what?" Harry Beest replied, not believing what Topper Wyld had just told him.

"You heard me correctly, Harry," Wyld grinned, seated behind his desk, his fingertips touching under his chin. "He wants to cut out the brain of a man and put it into the body of a gorilla. Or so he told me when he called earlier tonight."

"A gorilla?" Beest had seen and heard lots of strange things growing up in Cape Noire but this one went straight to top of the list. "Even if he could do that, where the hell is he going to get his hands on a gorilla?"

"Apparently he acquired one from a rundown traveling circus in Oregon. Seems their gorilla had become vicious over the past few months and killed several of the show's workers. Bugosi heard of this and offered the owner a considerable sum of money to purchase it and relieve him of his headache.

"And might I add, it was my money he used."

"So, you think he can actually do it...I mean put a fella's brains in an animal like that?"

"Who can say," Wyld shrugged, lowering his hands. "We've both seen his recent successes with making werewolves."

"Don't remind me, Boss. I know those things may come in handy for us, but I still don't like having to deal with them. It's just too creepy for my taste."

Wyld understood Beest's weariness. Bugosi was a genius. Of that there could be no question. But his experiments were bordering on insanity. He just hoped he could keep the eccentric scientist in line and focused on those projects Wyld would employ in his plans to become the sole king of Cape Noire.

It was time to move on to more pressing matters.

"So, Harry, is tonight's mission all set?"

"Yes, sir. Several of my guys scouted Cardigan's place and it shouldn't be a problem. He's only got a half-dozen men on hand at any given time."

"Good. And you've picked your men for the hit?"

"Yeah. Figure I'd take along Vengel, Bruno, Baldy Dave, Fox and the twins. Seven of us should be more than enough to get the job done."

"Fine. Cardigan's been getting too big for his own fat head lately and if what Wiseman tells me is true, he's all set to join Big Swede's operations. We can't let that happen. Big Swede's unchecked ambitions continue to portray me as weak on the streets. It's all orchestrated and if I don't act, it will embolden my enemies to unite against me.

"Which is why tonight's attack must be complete. I don't want any survivors, Harry. Understood?"

"Loud and clear, Boss." Harry started to get out of his chair.

"Tell me" Wyld raised a hand to delay him. "How are Jack and Tommy doing? Your reports have been extremely positive. You think they're ready for something like this?"

"Boss, the two love nothing better than mixing it up. Since giving them the numbers rackets on the east side, our take has doubled in the past few months. They had to break a few heads to make their presence felt, but pretty soon all the other bookies in that area were eager to work with them."

"Ha, that's what I like to hear," Wyld clapped his hands. "Initiative. And I'm not forgetting that's mostly due to your mentoring them, Harry. You've done an excellent job in bringing those boys along."

"They both have talent for our line of work. All I've done is just direct it. They're become known on the streets as the Bone Brothers and that tag is working for them."

"Very well, I won't keep you. Continue what you've been doing with them with my blessings. And report back to me when tonight's job is done. See to it that all your men get a nice bonus in their next weekly pay."

"Will do, Boss. Thanks." Beest stood and exited.

Closing the door behind him, he heard a distinct feminine curse. "Damn it all, not another run."

At the end of the hall, Alexis Wyld stood at the foot of the stairs, one leg posed on the second step, her plaid skirt pulled back to reveal a very shapely leg as she ran her hands along the silk stocking exploring the tear that went up her calve. "And they're supposed to be the best on the market!"

Harry Beest stood transfixed, eyeing the beautiful young woman before him. Topper Wyld's only child had matured into a raven-haired goddess, her body ripening in all the right ways from her long, elegant legs to her trim waist and generous bosom. Beest admired all these assets but it was her face that mesmerized him. From the classically sculptured jaw line, to her full lips, perfect nose and fiery green eyes under slim, pointed lashes. Her long shiny black hair reminded him of a lion's mane, seeming to frame her cold, captivating charms.

It was hard for him to reconcile the temptress he now gazed upon and the gawky, clumsy teenage girl who had once spied on him and her former nanny. It was as if nature had worked its own magic transforming a measly little worm into a truly gorgeous butterfly. One that now boldly glared back at him.

"See something you like, Harry?" he said, catching him ogling her leg.

Her taunting query snapped him out of his reverie and he casually walked over to her. "That and a whole lot more, kid."

Alexis dropped her skirt and stood with her hands folded over her chest. "Think you're pretty sure of yourself, don't you?"

"If by that you mean I'm not about to let some cocky little virgin get me in hot water with her father. Count on it. You can ply your wares to some other sucker. I'm not buying."

To that Alexis Wyld dropped her hands to her hips and purposely leaned in closer to him. Close enough where he could smell the delicate scent of her perfume. Her green eyes bore into him.

"You don't fool me for a second, Harry." Her jade colored eyes challenged him. "I know you'd love to do to me what you did to Yvette. And I'm ready and willing when you get up the courage."

Beest suddenly grabbed her by the shoulders and pushed her against the stairs. "Oh no you don't, sweetheart. I know this game all too well. And like I said, I'm not gonna let some sex obsessed little virgin jinx me. Not now and not ever."

Alexis laughed, shaking free of his grip. "Virgin! Oh, Harry, what you don't know about me. Before she left, Yvette told me all about sex. How to please any man. She said you were a good lover, but she'd had better."

Beest knew she was only trying to rankle him. Although he had been dismayed with Yvette Minault's resignation two years earlier upon Alexis' turning sixteen and moved on to another position out of town. Their love making had been great and with her gone, he hadn't picked up with anyone else. Like his men, the occasional visit to Madam Sadie's was enough to keep him satisfied in that category.

Satisfied, that is, until Wyld's own daughter, upon turning eighteen, had started coming on to him. At first he'd considered her antics amusing, but the more she pushed herself at him, the more his mind began to fantasize about seducing the daring Miss Wyld. It was a dangerous fantasy he simply couldn't give in to. Topper Wyld cherished the girl and if Beest, or any other of his men dared to lay a hand on her, the consequences would be lethal. Wyld's fatherly revenge would have no bounds.

"Look, kid. Cut it out, okay?" he started to back away from her. "Go play with the boys at that business college of yours and leave me the hell alone."

Before she could fire off another sarcastic remark, Harry Beest spun on his heels and marched away as fast as his legs would go.

I really don't need this kind of shit! No freakin' way!

Jack Bonello rolled over and his right hand came in contact with a soft, round bosom. He opened his eyes slowly, the light on the bed table allowing him to admire the fully naked breast on which it rested comfortably. For a second his eyes went from the semi-rigid nipple to the tattoo of a black ace that was displaced on his hand. He had a quick memory of Tommy and he at the tattoo parlor, with Harry Beest giving them the privilege of choosing what body art would forever distinguish the two of them. For the benefit of others of course. The boys already knew who they were. Anyway, he sighed, squeezing the woman's tit gently. He had opted for the black ace while Tommy had picked a devilish red skull. Thus it was no surprise to Beest that both boys had gone with symbols of death as if it had been pre-ordained at their birth that their lives would always be surrounded by blood and guts.

In the intervening years, under Beest's tutelage, Jack and Tommy had caused a great deal of mayhem. They'd also savagely eliminated nearly two dozen of Topper Wyld's enemies. Most of the bodies buried out in the woods west of Cape Noire in an area known only to them and Beest. As he'd reported to Wyld early on, the boys had a flair for killing and they relished every single hit they performed.

Bonello's bed mate began to squirm in her sleep and he gently pinched her pink nipple and the idea of waking her for another hot coupling was also awakening another part of his anatomy.

Which was when someone in the hall started banging on the door.

"Hey, Jack, wake up in there!" Tommy Bonello yelled so as to be heard clearly through the door. "We got twenty minutes before Harry picks us up and you know damn well how he doesn't like to be kept waiting."

"Wha—dah—?" the full bodied hooker rolled over to face Jack as he removed his hands from her breast. He smiled back at her and then sat up and threw the covers off his naked body.

"Sorry, Candy, but I gotta go to work."

He grabbed his clothes off the chair next to the bed, quickly donned his socks, pants and shirt before slipping his expensive Oxfords over his feet.

"Jack, you up in there?" Tommy was persistent if nothing else.

Jack ripped opened the door. "I'm up," he announced the obvious. "Now give me a second to finish getting dressed. Go on downstairs and I'll meet you there in a couple of minutes."

"All right," Tommy Bonello acquiesced. "But hurry it up."

As the door slammed shut, Tommy started back down the hall on the second floor of the fancy Victorian. He always felt eerie walking through the bordello's long hallway as it was lighted with red light bulbs supposedly to give the place a sensual ambience. It only reminded Tommy of blood.

"Who in tarnation is making all the damn noise in my house?" Madame Sadie Levine cursed, opening the door to her suite just as Bonello was passing by. Upon seeing him, she shook her head knowingly. Her hair was bound up in rollers and she was tugging on her heavy cotton housecoat.

"I might have known," she sneered. "You two boys can't do anything like normal folks. Got to come in my cathouse shouting and raising a ruckus as if the damn devil was having a party."

"Ah, relax Sadie. I just had to get Jack out of Candy's room. We got a job to do for the boss."

At the mention of their mutual employer, Sadie's face softened. "Well, all right, but try to keep it quiet going out. You know my customers don't like to be disturbed when they is here."

"We won't make another peep," Tommy grinned and pulled the brim of his fedora as a friendly salute. "Good night, Miss Sadie."

She grimaced and closed the door on him.

As Tommy walked towards the stairs at the end of the corridor, he imagined his twin primping himself in front of the girl's bathroom mirror. Making sure his tie was properly knotted and running a comb through his straight thick hair. Of the two, Jack was extremely vain and he made the most of his handsome features. Both had erupted from puberty to stand six feet two inches in height, with lithe muscular physiques that possessed both power and grace. Whereas Tommy was content to merely look good in the expensive clothes they both wore, Jack never tired of preening himself like a peacock. Which only made Tommy laugh.

Coming down the stairs to the main lounge he wasn't surprised to see it

"GOOD NIGHT, MISS SADIE."

occupied with only a few of Sadie's girls. Most were upstairs entertaining clients; the rich and powerful of the city. Seated on various sofas dressed in their lingerie, the others occupied themselves reading magazines, listening to the radio or playing cards. There was a grand piano in the right corner, but it being almost two in the morning, the black pianist Henry had long since retired for the evening. His normal work hours being eight to midnight.

Tommy went through the empty kitchen and out the back door where he plunked himself down on the top step of the veranda and lit up a cigarette. Blowing smoke into the night air, he looked at the surrounding neighborhood and for a moment appreciated the stillness. The houses to either side of the bordello were asleep with not a light in any of them. Decent folks didn't stay up all night like whores and gangsters. It wasn't often the hardened young killer gave much thought to such philosophical ideas.

Continuing to drag on his cigarette, he reflected on how well life had become for him and Jack ever since they'd signed on with Topper Wyld. True to his word, they had been handed a life of luxury and now only ate the best foods, drove the newest cars and had all the sex they could want with the most beautiful girls in town. It was a pretty cushy life and Tommy Bonello wouldn't have changed any of it.

Just as he exhaled another cloud of tobacco smoke, he heard footsteps behind him, then the screen door opening to let him know Jack had arrived.

"See, I told you not to sweat it," his brother declared tipping Tommy's hat off his head. Tommy caught it with one hand and as he was putting it back on, two sedans drove up from a side alley.

"And just in time," Tommy flipped the remainder of his butt into the night as he got to his feet.

The lead car was a Buick and in the front seat Harry Beest sat on the passenger side while the small, rat-faced Reed Vengel was behind the wheel. As the Bonello brothers walked over and started to climb into the back seat, Tommy recognized the passengers in the Studebaker that had followed the Buick. Bruno St. George was the driver with Baldy Dave sitting beside him. Though he couldn't make out the third rider in their back seat, he rightly assumed it was Arnie Britwell.

"You boys ready?" Beest asked, looking back at the twins and giving Vengel the sign to move out.

"You bet, Harry," Jack grinned sitting back and making himself comfortable. "Time to go have some real fun."

Tommy pointed both of his index fingers and mouthed, "Boom, boom, here come the Bonello Brothers."

Beest started to laugh and turned to watch the road ahead.

CHAPTER (17)

Dick Cardigan lived in a two story house North West of the city near the village of Castle Harbor. It being long after midnight, the two vehicles carrying Topper Wyld's men encountered very little traffic driving to the locale. The house was located at the end of road, its back set against a copse of pine trees beyond which the waters of the shore were visible on a good day. At night all that could be heard was the constant crashing of the surf as it hit the beaches.

Harry Beest had Revenge El kill the lights the second they arrived on the street. A half moon hanging overhead and a few sparsely set street lamps were enough to illuminate the sparsely populated neighborhood. The Studebaker following them also went dark. Beest counted only three houses to either side as they approached Cardigan's place and smiled. The fewer people to interfere or call the cops when the shooting started.

Beest directed Vengel to stop half a block from the darkened abode. There were two sedans parked in the driveway and a third against the sidewalk curb blocking the front entrance. As he, Vengel and the Bonellos exited their car, Beest went around to the back and popped the trunk. Inside, resting against a thick canvas sheet were several Thompson machine-guns and two short-barrel shotguns.

"Pick your poison," he grinned.

Both Jack and Tommy eagerly grabbed for the Tommy guns and hefted them up to their chests enjoying the feel of their hard metal in their hands. The small Reed Vengel opted for one of the shotguns while Beest watched silently. All of them knew he preferred his twin .45 automatics hidden beneath his coat in shoulder holsters.

As the armed killers stepped back from the car, Beest quietly dropped the trunk cover. From the back end of the Studebaker, the remaining three gunmen joined them. Bruno St. George was a square shouldered thug with a rough-hewn face. He wielded a Tommy gun as did Baldy Dave Jackman, a tall man with a thick black beard most assumed he'd let grown upon losing his hair on top. Lastly the dapper, well-dressed Arnie Britwell with the round face and glasses, hefted a sawed-off 12 gauge shotgun.

Once assembled, Harry Beest leaned in and whispered their orders.

"Baldy, you and Jack go around the house and get set up in the backyard. You've got five minutes."

At that, Jack turned and gave Beest a sour look. He and Tommy generally worked together side by side. It was only recently that Beest had purposely begun separating the brothers. His reasoning being that their dependence on each other would one day be a serious liability that might get one or both of them killed. Still it didn't mean they liked the prospect of being apart when bullets started to fly. Thus Jack's glaring look.

"You got a problem with that, Jack?" Beest asked directly.

For a second Jack looked to Tommy and then shook his head slightly. "Nah, no problem, Harry."

"Good. I repeat, we'll give you both five minutes to set up. Then the rest of us will come in the front door blasting way. Once the shooting starts, any of Cardigan's men try to get out that way, you two take care of them. Mister Wyld said no one gets out. Got that?"

"Gotcha," Baldy Dave nodded, his black knit cap reminding them of the sailor he'd once been before settling in Cape Noire. He turned to Jack and slapped him on the arm. "Let's go, kid. Time to get this party started."

They jogged away nearing the house that was their target and veered off around the bushes that skirted the property and were soon lost in the blackness beyond.

The others looked at Beest, as he quietly stood gazing at the sleeping domicile before them. He was mentally working out the seconds and minutes that allowed for Dave and Jack to reach their rear guard position.

Finally he looked at his men, opened his coat and pulled out his two automatics holding them up, ready to use. It was all the signal they needed. Beest started down the middle of the street with the other four right behind him. Each held their weapons tightly, their eyes surveying the darkened neighborhood ever watchful for any unexpected surprise.

Which is exactly what they received when almost at Cardigan's driveway the night's stillness was shattered by the loud barking of a dog. Beest and his crew froze, each man looking around frantically. As the barking continued, it became obvious it was coming from behind one of the houses behind them. Most likely some animal chained in a backyard and with its sensitive hearing had easily been awakened by their presence.

And now it was making an endless ruckus that Beest knew would ultimately rouse everyone nearby including Cardigan and his people.

No sooner had the thought crossed his mind when a light went on in one of the upstairs windows.

"Shit," he blurted out. The die was cast. Unless they moved fast, their opportunity to catch Cardigan and his men unprepared would evaporate like rain drops on a hot summer sidewalk.

"Hurry it up!" he now commanded, increasing his own pace to reach the front door. The others kept up with him and once at the portal, Beest turned to Vengel and waved one of his guns at the brass door knob. Needing no further instructions, the small gangster planted his feet firmly, pointed the end of his shot gun directly at the knob and pulled one of the triggers. The blast was loud and the lead pellets tore the knob away blowing a fist size hole in the wood.

Beest kicked the ruined door in and entered the darkened house, his pistols leading the way. In the gloom of what he saw as a living room, two human figures were scrambling out of chairs, their arms seeming to claw at their sides for something. Something he knew were their own handguns.

He fired both automatics at the same time punching holes in Cardigan's men, the bullets rocking them off their feet. The confines of the room made the gunshots deafening and Beest, knowing fully well Cardigan had more than these two men he'd taken down, was doing his best to stay sharp and alert. Their voices. Lots of voices coming from various parts of the house.

By now Vengel, St. George and Tommy Bonello had come into the house, with Arnie Britwell still on the front stoop.

"Don't bunch together," Beest warned just as two more shapes appeared from what was obviously a hallway to their right. Then, before he could fire at them, there was a tiny snap and the overhead lights went on blinding him momentarily.

"Look out!" Bruno St. George standing behind him shouted and shoved Beest aside as Cardigan's men opened up on them. Bullets rang out and St. George felt one tear across the top of his shoulder, ripping his jacket while another went past his right ear. Screaming at the top of his lungs, he leveled the Tommy gun in his mitts and squeezed the trigger.

Hot lead blazed across the room catching the two gunmen like a line of mini shredders tearing across their bodies, ripping dozens of holes into them. Blood spurted everywhere as the doomed hoods danced like crazed marionettes whose puppet chords had been violently jerked free. They collapsed to the floor, their lives forfeited in the space of a few seconds.

At the first shots fired downstairs, Dick Cardigan jumped out of his bed and pulled the drawer open on the small side table. He'd been awakened by his neighbor's dog barking up a storm. He was familiar with that big German Shepherd and knew it wouldn't have let something like a squirrel or rabbit disturb its slumber. So he'd reached out and turned on the table lamp seconds before the barrage of fire invaded his home.

Gladys, his wife, was sitting up still half asleep but the look in her eyes revealed the dawning of real fear.

"Dick?"

"Shh…get out of bed honey," he told her, moving to the bedroom door, his .38 Smith & Wesson revolver in hand and wearing only his blue striped pajama bottom. He pulled the door open and ventured into the hall as Gladys came up behind him tieing her nightgown about her.

More shots echoed up from below and she clutched his arm. Again he put a finger over his lips and led her to the children's room. They found their seven year old son Dick Junior standing in between the two twin beds holding hands with his five year old brother Paul. Both looked confused and scared.

"Mommy," Paul rushed to Gladys and wrapped his arms around her legs. She bent down and lifted him into her arms.

"Be quiet," Cardigan told his sons, as he took Junior by the shoulder and once again went back out into the hall. At the end to their right was a linen closet and that was where he brought them. He opened the door, grabbed one of the shelves covered with sheets and blankets and pushed it hard. There was a squeaking noise and the entire wall opened into a small dark alcove and a hidden staircase to the kitchen below.

"Don't turn on the lights," he cautioned Gladys as he ushered her past him still clutching Paul to her. Then he looked down at Dick Junior and nodded. "You take care of your mother and brother. Got that?"

"I will, Papa."

"Good, now all of you get going. Make for the woods and wait there until it's safe."

He leaned into Gladys and kissed her once and then as they started to descend the hidden stairs, he pulled the false wall closed.

Taking a deep breath, Dick Cardigan returned to the hallway and in a crouch moved towards the stairs and whatever chaos awaited him below.

Bullets ripped into the wall destroying framed photographs over Harry Beest's head as he hid behind a stuffed chair. Pieces of glass and plaster rained down on his fedora and shoulders. Two more of Cardigan's goons were backed against a stairwell desperately firing round after round to stall Beest and his invading force.

To his right, Arnie Britwell was folded behind a thick padded sofa as bullets tore the stuffing out of it. Ultimately it wouldn't be enough to stop the bullets and he knew it. St. George and Tommy Bonello had disappeared to the left part of the house and they could hear their Tommy guns chattering away. Beest had directed them to check out the cellar while he and Britwell continued going through the main floor.

Britwell's glasses had slipped down his nose and he started to push them back when a bullet tore the fedora off his head. His eyes doubled in size and looking across the room at Beest, he swore loudly. "I've had enough of this bullshit."

He sprang to his feet, his Thompson submachine ready and let loose a volley at the two shooters who had been keeping them pinned down. Beest couldn't believe the guy's recklessness—only in this case it paid off. His shots were on target sending multiple rounds into Cardigan's men. They yelled out in pain and were tossed to the floor like rag dolls.

Looking over the chair back, Beest saw them fall and jumped to his feet. He started to race over to stairs at the same time the light from the parlor behind him showed him a pair of bare feet descending.

Then Dick Cardigan was half way down the stairs and upon seeing Harry Beest, both of them fired at each other wildly.

Beest's aim was quick and true as he shot Cardigan dead center of his chest. At the same time he caught the flash muzzle of Cardigan's revolver and there was a blinding stab of pain.

I've been shot! was his last conscious thought.

Jack Bonello was getting fidgety what with hearing all the shooting going on inside the house and the constant yelping of that dog. The animal had never ceased its barking and once the gunfire had begun, the creature had seemed more intent upon waking up the entire block. Not that the gun battle wouldn't be doing that soon enough.

And here he and Baldy Dave Jackman were, standing between the back of the building and the dense woods.

"What the da hells going on in there?" he asked Jackman.

The older thug merely shrugged while holding his Tommy gun aimed at the ground. Thus far there had been no activity from the back windows to either side of the porch. Jackman wasn't a talker, which irritated Jack a bit. It was as if he was always in control of his emotions. Never anxious to do anything. A good, steady soldier as how the Bonello twin thought of the bearded mobster.

He was about to suggest they try and open the back door themselves when suddenly it sprung open as if on its own. Jack blinked, whipping up his weapon.

Coming out of the house was a woman clutching a child in her arms and leading a second one. They reached the first cement step of the porch when she spotted the Topper Wyld's hitmen.

"NO!" she gasped, putting her right hand down on the oldest boy trying to push him behind her.

Jack Bonello turned the Tommy gun on them as a cruel smile appeared on his lips.

"Please," Gladys Cardigan begged just before he squeezed the trigger.

The roar of the machine gun filled the night along with her scream and within three seconds ravished the mother and her children until they are strewn on the ground having fallen off the wooden platform upon being slaughtered.

Their bodies were unmoving, blood seeping from dozens of wounds.

"Jesus!" Dave Jackman gulped. "They were just kids!" He looked at Jack Bonello seeing him as if for the very first time.

"Yeah, so what?" Jack chuckled. "Just doing what we were told to do, Dave. You got a problem with that?"

Jackman felt his stomach twist and thought he was going to be sick. He'd done a lot of bad things in his life, including murder. But never once had he ever harmed children. That was beyond his personal moral sense of right and wrong. And now Jack was laughing about as if it was a joke of some kind. What kind of sick twisted bastard was he?

At that moment a light went on in the kitchen and another person started coming out of the back door. Both Dave and Jack started to fire only to see it was Tommy Bonello waving his right hand up in the air.

"Guys!" he shouted. "Get in here. Harry's been shot!"

CHAPTER (18)

Detective Dan Rains hadn't worked the night shift in years. That had been back in the days when he first earned his gold shield. Since then he'd been promoted twice up to third grade level, designated Detective Inspector. He thought of this as he drove his unmarked sedan along the isolated street just as the first rays of twilight began piercing the overhead sky with shafts of purple and pink. It was now five-forty and the sun would soon be claiming its throne in only a few more minutes. It was much too beautiful a vista for the horror he was on his way to witness.

The call had come in a half hour earlier. The night squad, along with several patrol cars had responded and discovered the massacre at the Cardigan home. After a radio alert back to headquarters, the Duty Sergeant took it upon himself to call Rains and get him out of bed early. That's why he knew it was bad.

The end of the street was blocked off by wooden sawhorses beyond which were parked three police cars, another unmarked vehicle and two white ambulances with their lights flashing were actually backed up on the front lawn. Rains could see the front door was wide open with cops and hospital people milling about. Every single light in the house had been lit and the new crime scene displayed its own brightly gruesome appearance.

As he neared the blockade, Rains spotted several of the neighbors to either side of the small street outside in their robes curious to see what had transpired. One man was holding on to the leash of a big gray German Shepherd dog that was barking while attempting to break free of its collar.

It's like he smells the dead, Rains reflected coming to a halt in the middle of the road where two sawhorses met. A uniformed officer behind the barrier recognized him and hastily picked up the end of one of the wooden constructs. He pulled it back allowing Rains' car enough room to drive through.

The Detective Inspector parked away from all the other automobiles and made his way around those parked in the driveway; obviously belonging to the inhabitants. As he neared the front entrance, two white coated attendants emerged carrying a sheet-covered body on a canvas stretcher. As they carefully walked down the steps, one of them looked at Sgt. Terrence Duseault posted by the door. "That's the first one," he said.

"How many more in there?" Duseault asked the obvious question.

"At least eight or nine," the ambulance driver replied. "We're going to have to make several trips."

Once at the hospital van, the two men carefully maneuvered the stretcher to slide it into the back before carefully lifting the body and setting it down against the side wall. Then it was back into the house with the stretcher empty and ready for another passenger.

"Looks like a mess," Dan Rains commented as he arrived.

"Inspector," Sgt. Duseault smiled. "Good to see you, sir. Guess they kicked you out of bed, huh?"

Rains nodded. "Yup. And good to see you too, Terry. I hear you're doing right by those stripes on your arm."

Rains' old friend, Officer Terrence Duseault had been promoted to Sergeant shortly after his own upgrade and then been transferred to the Castle Harbor station. Consequently they hadn't seen each other in over two years. Rains would have enjoyed getting caught up with Duseault, but this simply wasn't the time or place.

"Hey," a voice rang out from inside the house. "Is that Rains? Get your ass in here."

Rains grinned at the Sergeant. "Duty beckons. Maybe we can get a coffee later."

"I'd like nothing better, Dan."

Rains entered the front vestibule in time to avoid the second pair of ambulance personnel rushing for the door with another stretcher-bound corpse. He found himself in what was left of the living room. All the furniture had been destroyed and most of it was lying strewn about the area. Bullet holes adorned all the walls and between the dead bodies he carefully stepped over were congealed pools of blood. All he could think of while doing so were the trenches in France he'd survived long, long ago. He had hoped to never see that kind of carnage again.

Right. Welcome to Cape Noire.

A flashbulb went off to his right and he looked down a corridor to see Jeff Nolan, the police photographer, pointing his box camera down at another three dead men scattered along the floor.

"Hi, Inspector," the cameraman acknowledge as he removed a spent bulb in its casing and replaced with a new one he'd removed from his jacket pocket.

"Nolan." He glanced around. "Walters and Ham here?"

"We're in the kitchen," Detective Sam Walters' voice spoke a second time. "Straight ahead, Rains."

Rains followed the sound, reached the door and pushed it wide. In the tight, square kitchen he found the two night shift bulls standing by the back door. Walters was of average height, with a long jaw, and a pencil thin mustache under his nose. His partner, Luke Hamerstand, nicknamed Ham, was a stout, beefy type with a bulbous nose. He always wore a round, silly porkpie hat. At the sight of Rains, he turned away from the open door. There was activity outside, but the Inspector couldn't see it yet.

"Sorry to disturb your beauty sleep," Ham offered, jokingly. He was holding a notepad and pencil. "Figured the Captain would want you or Serat to take over here. Guess you got the short end of the stick eh, Rains."

"So is seems." Rains shrugged. Considering how *in* with the Captain Detective Lt. Clement Serat was, it was surprise he had been the one called. "Looks like a gang hit."

"He's a regular Sherlock Holmes," Sam Walters told his partner. He had a high pitched voice that got on people's nerves. "What gave you a clue, Rains?"

Rains ignored the jibe. He'd learned long ago that most cops resorted to juvenile humor when confronted with the results of brutal violence. It was a defense mechanism which made it possible for them to cope with the things they saw. The stuff of nightmares.

"Whose place is this?" he asked.

Ham answered. "A low-level mug named Dick Cardigan. According the word on the street, he was an up-and-coming player and was hoping to join forces with Big Swede Jorgenson."

"Guess that's not going to happen now?" Rains looked around the kitchen. "Is he in the house someplace?"

"Out in the hall," Walters reported. "Down at the foot of the stairs. Looks like a Tommy gun did the job."

Rains pointed past his colleagues to the backyard slowly dispelling the shadows of the night. "What's out there?"

Ham shook his head as if trying to erase the memory of what he and Walters had come upon only fifteen minutes early. "See for yourself."

Dan Rains walked out onto the porch and saw what was left of Gladys Cardigan and her boys. Another ambulance attendant was in the process of covering them with new, starched sheets.

Rains had no words.

Butch Hammer was sweeping the sidewalk in front of the Gridiron Saloon, enjoying the warmth of the sun. It was almost noon and business was steady if not great. He assumed it would pick up after lunch time. At present his wife Peggy was handling the bar and the few customers they had.

"Hi ya, Butch," Baldy Dave Jackman came walking up the sidewalk. He was a regular and though Hammer knew he was a mob guy, he liked the big, bald oaf with the thick black beard like the Smith Brothers on the cough-drop box. "How's business?"

At that Jackman chuckled. "Well, let's get inside and you can get me some grub and a drink then."

"Fair enough." Hammer looked at the cleared off sidewalk and decided he was done. "This is as good as it's going to get."

He pulled the door open ushered his customer inside. Jackman went to the bar and sat on one of the empty stools at the center. Peggy, who had been cleaning glasses in the sink, greeted him with a smile.

"What can I get you, Dave? A beer?"

Jackman ran a hand over his beard giving the question extra thought before surprising her. "You got any fresh coffee back there in the kitchen?"

"Always. You want a cup?"

"As long as you pour in a shot of Jameson's," he added.

"Ha," she laughed. "Anything else? We've got a couple of donuts left that Butch picked up from Delmont's Bakery this morning."

"Yeah, that sounds just fine. Thanks, Peggy."

"No problem." She dropped her cleaning towel next to the under-the-counter sink and went into the kitchen to get his order.

Meanwhile Butch Hammer had stowed his broom away in the cleaning closet next to the glassed-in phone booth and was walking along the row of tables when the back door opened and his mother-in-law, Molly McCoy, appeared with her ever-present hardwood cane in her right hand and his three year old son, Rafe holding on to her left. The second Rafe looked up and saw his father, he pulled free of Molly and raced down the aisle, arms out flung.

"Daddy!"

Hammer dropped down and scooped up the curly-headed little scamp, his own joyous smile matching his son's.

How the hell did I get so lucky? It was a question he'd asked himself a million times since Rafe's birth. And all of it had started five years earlier when Molly had suffered her stroke. For a long while, it was thought she would never walk again; her right leg and arm having been paralyzed. But Molly McCoy was a fighter in every sense of the word and told Butch and Peggy she wasn't about to spend her remaining time on this earth tied to a wheelchair. True to her word, she had accepted the physical therapy program established by her doctors and within six months of the stroke, she was able to get about with two canes. She reminded Hammer of a aged little mountain skier seeing her move around the bar with her sticks holding her up.

As the days and months passed, Molly only got stronger until not only did she regain complete function of her right arm, but the leg also began to show signs of healing. Though the doctors agreed she'd never lose the limp she'd acquired, as long as she kept the one cane, there was no reason she couldn't continue her normal activities. Within reason, of course.

Which was when Peggy and Butch told her of their intentions to wed. For an old Irish immigrant, it was the best news ever and on their wedding day, she gave them the bar as a wedding gift. "Providing you don't ever kick me out," she'd finished, enjoying the look of surprise on their faces. Even Father O'Malley, the pastor at St. Michael's Catholic Church enjoyed the moment.

Ten months later Peggy Hammer gave birth to Rafe Aaron Hammer. Rafe had been the name of Molly's deceased husband and Peggy's father. When she was told what the new babe would be christened, the waterworks had begun.

And that was three years ago! Swinging Rafe around in his arms, Hammer couldn't believe how fast time had flown by.

"That your boy?" Dave Jackman said, turning on his stool.

"Indeed he is," Hammer replied. "And he's a chip off the old block."

"That he is," Molly McCoy agreed. "And then some. Takes after my late lamented husband, the one and only, the saints keep him."

"I'm a chip," little Rafe echoed. "Off the block. Eh, Daddy."

"Don't go making him dizzy again," Peggy warned coming out of the kitchen with a hot cup of black coffee generously laced with whiskey and a tray holding two large donuts. She set it front of Baldy Dave. "You made him throw up his supper last time you rough-housed with him like that."

"Come on, Peggy, it was only the one time. Right, Rafy boy."

"Rafy boy," the child repeated laughing as he father continued to whirl him around. The other few customers in the booths all smiled.

"Oh, that's just what the doctor ordered," Jackman said, smacking his lips after taking a big gulp. "Thanks, Peggy." Then he devoured half a donut in one bite. It was as if he hadn't eaten in days.

Hammer heard the door open behind him and looked over his shoulder to see Betty One-Eye walk in followed by her tall black ball-buster, Eli St. John. Both of them were familiar figures on the docks of Old Town. Hammer had heard lots of nasty things about the two of them, but thus far they had never given him any trouble, so he had no problems with them frequenting the Gridiron. At one time Betty One-Eye had two leg-breakers and then one day one of them was gone. As Hammer recalled he'd been a foreigner from Mongolia. Word on the street was divided on that situation. One group said he'd merely had enough with Cape Noire and sailed back to his own country. The other party suspected he'd been gunned down in one of Betty's regular altercations with another rival gang and was now buried somewhere in the deep woods west of the city.

Again, Butch Hammer could care less as long as she and her pals behaved. The last thing he ever wanted was trouble. Both because of his past and now that he had a family to look after.

"So how's the little the rascal doing today?" Betty One-Eye laughed as she approached Hammer. She started to reach out a hand towards the boy and his face immediately scrunched up in fear. He began to cry and sought to bury his face in his father's shoulder.

"Back off," Molly McCoy ordered, stepping up to her son-in-law and lifting her cane to point at the patch-wearing redhead. "Don't you be scaring my grandson, Beatrice Ann McCauley, or you'll rue the day you crossed my path."

"Aw, stuff it, you old wind bag," Betty retorted. "I was only trying to be friendly to the wee one."

"He won't be needing your kind of friendship," Molly spat.

"Whoa there," Butch interrupted before things got out of hand. He knew Molly's temper when her hackles were up and she'd never liked Big Swede Jorgenson's lady. Not one little bit. "Let's all calm down here." He handed Rafe over to his mother-in-law just as Peggy materialized across the bar and gave him an inquisitive look.

"Bring Rafe to his mother," Butch said, and then gave Betty One-Eye and Eli St. John a smile he hoped was neutral. "What can I get you two? Beers?"

"Yeah, that sounds good, Butch." Betty pointed to the empty booth a few feet away. "We'll take that booth over. And if you've got any pretzels, send them along too."

"Will do."

As the pair moved away, Hammer sighed and went to pour their beers. Meanwhile Molly had taken Rafe into the kitchen where Peggy had given him a donut covered with powered sugar. Within seconds the white stuff was all over his lips and lower jaw. At the same time Baldy Dave Jackman finished his pastry and drink and was in the process of digging out a wrinkled dollar from his pants pocket to square his bill.

"Hey, Baldy." Betty One-Eye had seen him slide off his stool and now waved to him. "Come on over and join Eli and me."

"Ah, I really don't have much time," he tried to beg off.

"You got time for one beer," she argued. "On me. Come on, what's the rush?"

Having no better excuse, Jackman nodded and started over at the same time Hammer came over and deposited two mugs of foaming beer on the table.

"Get us one more, will ya, Butch," Betty said, as Jackman moved around him and slid onto the padded bench next to St. John.

"So what you been up to?" Betty asked pulling a cigarillo out of her shirt pocket. "I heard poor Dick Cardigan and his crew got put down last night." She struck a wooden match on the table top and held it to the tip of her thin smoke. "You wouldn't know anything about that, would you Baldy?"

"You know better than that, Betty," Jackman squirmed doing his best to stay calm. "I don't know squat. Okay."

She laughed and blew out a dirty cloud of gray smoke. "Sure, Baldy, sure. You're no rat. But I got to ask, how you like working under a lowlife like Harry Beest? I hear he don't take no crap from anybody."

"Aw, Harry's all right. It's Mr. Wyld's two new boys that give me the creeps."

"You mean the twins?"

"Yeah. Tommy and Jack."

"The Bone Brothers," Betty took a sip of her beer. "They as mean as they say?"

Jackman started to reply when Hammer appeared and put a down a mug of beer before him. "Here you go, Baldy." In his other hand he held a bowl filled with the pretzels that Betty-One aye had requested. He set them before her.

"Thanks Butch." She blew out another puff of cigar smoke.

Once the bartender walked off, Jackman took a long drink of his beer. He loved the bitter taste of the hops. Finished, he set the glass down.

"You was saying?" Betty One-Eye reminded him as she picked up a pretzel and began munching on it. "About the Bone Brothers."

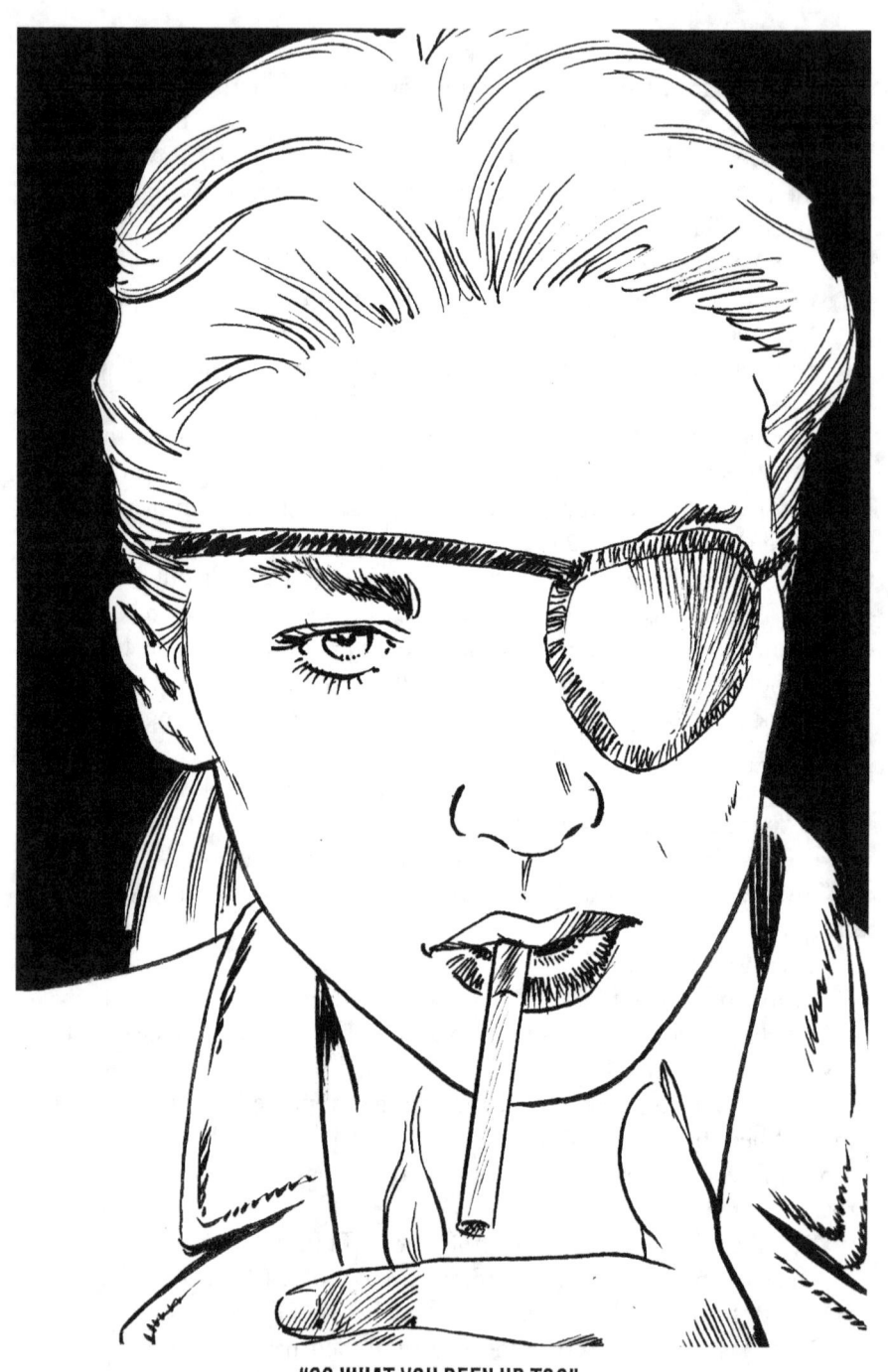

"SO WHAT YOU BEEN UP TO?"

"Oh, yeah." Jackman leaned over the table and declared, "They're animals, I tell you. Both of them goddamn, vicious animals."

Harry Beest had the champion of all headaches. It arrived with his consciousness and before he even opened his eyes, the pain that lanced through him was enough proof that he was still among the living. He blinked and opened his eyes.

"Ow."

He was in a bed, not his own, surrounded by familiar faces. He blinked again wishing the fire in his head to go away.

"Now take it slow, Harry." Doctor Ernest Athlon advised putting a firm restraining hand on Harry's left shoulder. The old man seated in a chair by the bed was Topper Wyld's long-time personal physician. Harry had met the white-haired fellow on many occasions. "Don't try to raise your head."

"Whatever you say, Doc," Harry brought up his left hand and felt the stitches at the top of his forehead."

"You're a lucky bastard," Topper Wyld said, standing at the foot of the bed. "The doctor says another inch and a half lower and that slug would have ripped into your skull instead of skimming off the top of it as it did."

"If you say so, Boss. But right now it hurts like a sonofabitch."

Wyld chuckled as did Reed Vengel, who was standing next to him. Beest now realized he was in one of the mansion's many second floor guest bedrooms.

"Damn," Revenge El blurted out. "We thought sure as hell you were dead, Harry. All the blood running down your face in and on your head. We got you back here as fast as we could."

Beest closed his eyes for a second and mentally put it altogether. He wanted to ask Vengel how the rest of the hit had gone but knew better than to say anything in front of Doc Athlon.

"So I'm gonna live?" he asked opening his eyes again.

"Only if you leave those stitches alone," the doctor informed him as he pushed his chair back and stood up. "And stay in that bed for the next few days. Even though the bullet only creased your scalp, you still suffered a severe concussion and any strenuous activity may jeopardize your health."

"Rest assured, I'll see to it that he stays put," Topper Wyld declared. "I'll see that he gets all the care he requires."

No sooner had the words left his mouth then Alexis Wyld walked through the open door. "And I'll help too, Father." She came to stand between Wyld and Vengel, hands folded behind her back. She wore a beautiful dress with a colorful floral pattern in greens and yellows with a small brown belt.

Again, Beest was taken by her radiant beauty.

Doctor Athlon was putting on his suit coat before picking up his medical valise off the floor. "Good. I'm thinking Harry should have some soup when he feels up to it. No solids until after he's had a good night's sleep."

Alexis brought her hands together. "All right. I'll go down to the kitchen and get Chef Louis on that right now."

"Excellent, my dear," Wyld approved. "And at the same time be so good as to see the good doctor out."

"Of course, Father."

Wyld extended his right hand and the doctor shook it.

"Thank you, Doctor."

"Of course, Topper. If there are any complications, don't hesitate to call me."

"I will. Take care, my friend."

With that, Alexis stepped up and took the doctor's right arm, folded hers around it and together they exited the room.

Beest waited a few more minutes before speaking again. "How'd the hit go, El?"

"Like a piece of cake, Harry," the ferret-like gangster beamed. "By the time we left, there weren't a living soul in that place."

"And the boys?"

"All good. Bruno got a bullet scratch across the shoulder, but the Doc patched him up earlier. They're all okay."

"Indeed." Topper Wyld moved around the bed to take a position by the empty chair and look down at his chief enforcer with approval. "Now Big Swede is going to think twice before he attempts any other such frivolous unions.

"Good work, my boy. Now you close your eyes and get some rest."

"Thanks, Boss."

Beest watched Wyld and Vengel walk out the room and felt his eyes getting heavy again. Sleep sounded like a really good idea.

CHAPTER (19)

Big Swede Jorgenson picked up the phone on his desk, gave the operator the number he wished to reach and waited as she connected him. Seated across from him was one of his chief enforcers, Bill Morris, seated in a high-backed chair, one leg crossed over the other. A former dock worker, Morris had a rough face centered by a busted nose. He always appeared uncomfortable in the suits Jorgenson had him wear.

Now he was nervously smoking a Chesterfield cigarette awaiting his boss' next orders.

Jorgenson heard a click and then a soft, familiar voice. "Hello, Barrett Funeral Home, Leslie Barrett speaking."

"Good evening, Mr. Barrett. This is Nils Jorgenson."

"Mr. Jorgenson. Nice to hear from you, sir. How may I be of service?"

"I'm calling in regards to the horrendous tragedy that befell my late associate, Mr. Richard Cardigan and his wife and children."

There was a pause on the line before Barrett reacted. "A tragedy indeed. I was shaken to the core when I first read about it in the papers."

"Yes, well, I would like to have the family's remains brought to your funeral home and have you see to their care and final repose. Of course I'll pay for the services to include burial in a nice, local cemetery."

"Ah, well that's most generous of you, Mr. Jorgenson, but I'm afraid that won't be necessary."

Big Swede' back stiffened. "Oh, and why is that?"

"Someone else has already contacted us and made similar arrangements."

"I see. May I ask who that was?"

"Please understand, Mr. Jorgenson, it is not our policy to divulge such information as many of our clients wish to remain anonymous."

Big Swede could feel his blood pressure rising and he gritted his teeth.

"Mr. Barrett, need I remind you of our past dealings and the less than legal nature of those bodies that found their way into your establishment."

"Please, Mr. Jorgenson, I simply do not want to…"

"Who called you, Barrett?"

"Topper Wyld, sir. He called early this morning."

"WHAT!" Jorgenson pulled the receiver from his ear and glared at as if he hadn't heard what the nebbish undertaker had told him. Then slowly he put it back.

"Ah…I'm sorry, if I did anything wrong, Mr. Jorgenson. I mean, Mr. Wyld seemed genuinely sincere in wanting to handle the arrangements and—"

"Oh, I'm sure he did," Jorgenson growled sarcastically. "I'm sure he did. Good night, Mr. Barrett." He slammed the phone down hard startling Bill Morris who knew how dangerous his boss could be when he lost his temper.

"Something wrong, Mr. Jorgenson?"

"Wrong, I'll say there's something wrong!"

At that moment Betty One-Eye came walking into the office along with Eli St. John.

"Do tell, Big Swede," she grinned as she strolled up to his desk and sat on the corner. "What is it that has you seeing red and blowing steam out of your ears?"

"It's Wyld!" Jorgenson swung his chair around to address her. "That bastard had the balls to call the funeral home and take care of burying Cardigan and his brood."

"So?" The redhead peeled off one of her leather gloves seemingly amused by his ire.

"SO!" Jorgenson slammed his right hand on the desk. "It's all but a sure thing he orchestrated the hit and now he shoves it up my nose by footing bill for Cardigan's send-off. Word gets out on the street and it will humiliate me to the other gangs."

"Well, you are right about that first part," Betty was removing the second glove. "Eli and I ran into Baldy Dave Jackman this morning at the Grid Iron Saloon. He all but admitted it he was part of the crew that did the hit."

Big Swede pushed back in chair and pulled at his chin with his left hand. "Hmm, then it must have been Wyld's man, Harry Beest, who was in charge."

"Yeah, he and his junior grade killers, the Bone Brothers. However it went down, Baldy was shook up about it."

"Hmm," Jorgenson considered this new information. "I'm getting sick and tired of Topper Wyld thinking he runs this entire city."

"So do something about it," Betty suggested, slapping her gloves in the palm of her hand. "Just give me the word and me and the boys will knock him off that mountaintop of his."

"As much as I'd like nothing better, now isn't the time." He saw the disappointment in Betty's face. "We can't rush it, Baby. No, that's what that old bastard wants us to do. React stupidly without a real strategy."

Big Swede Jorgenson stood and put his hands together. "No, I won't let him goad me into moving until I know we're ready."

"So, when will that be?" Betty got off the desk.

"Soon, my love." Jorgenson came over and wrapped her in his arms. "Soon enough."

Harry Beest rinsed his razor under the hot water tap and examined his newly clean-shaven face in the bathroom mirror. He'd had Reed Vengel bring his kit from his apartment in the guest house the day before. He was well aware how Topper Wyld preferred having his people looking neat and clean. Five o'clock shadows were frowned upon. He was putting the razor away in its leather case when he heard someone enter the bedroom through the bathroom door.

"Harry?" Alexis Wyld called out. "You in there?"

"Yeah," he responded opening the door. He was barefooted in pajama pants and now had a bath towel draped around his neck. "I'm gonna take a bath."

Alexis held a food tray on which was a ham and cheese sandwich, a huge kosher dill pickle and an open bottle of beer. "I brought you some lunch."

She turned from him and went to set the tray down on the small table to the left of the bed. Wearing a knee-length gray skirt and blue satin blouse, she was a very pleasing vision as she bent over.

All woman, Beest thought as his mind entertained images of what was beneath that chic outfit.

As if reading his mind, Alexis turned and gave him a coy smile. She walked over to him and reached up to touch his face. "Now that's much better, Harry."

"I'm glad you approve." He could smell her lilac perfume. The nearness of her was tempting.

"Oh, I do." She inched closer. "More than you know."

Before he knew what was happening, the brunette temptress had reached up with her other hand and pulled his head down so that their lips would meet. Beest was startled and jerked his head away.

"What do you think you're doing?" he asked, flustered.

"Come now, Harry, don't tell me you didn't like that."

"That's the not the point, Alexis."

"Then what is?"

"You're off limits, sweetheart. You know that. Your old man would roast me alive if he thought for a second we were fooling around."

"Oh, Harry," she laughed softly. "Don't tell me you're afraid of Daddy."

"I'd be stupid not to be."

Alexis put both her hands on his naked chest and licked her lower lip. "Harry, I want you. And I think you want me too."

Her nails scratched across his skin and Beest cringed slightly. Her green eyes were on fire looking up at him and he knew he couldn't resist her. He grabbed her arms and instead of shoving her away this time, he pulled her to him and kissed her again. He kissed her hard, letting her know the hunger that was boiling up inside of him.

Alexis didn't shy away, breaking loose of his grip, she wrapped her own arms up around his neck and pressed her full breasts against him. Her lips never yielding, matching his desire with her own.

So caught up in the moment was Beest, he failed to hear the footsteps coming down the hall. But Topper Wyld's cough he did not miss. Instantly he pushed Alexis off him and brushed the back of his left hand over his lips hoping she hadn't left a trace of her lipstick.

The door opened and Topper Wyld, still coughing, entered. For a second he was surprised by his daughter's presence. She and Beest stood side by side next to the open bathroom door.

"Alexis…cough, there you are," he managed.

"Father, are you all right?"

"Oh, yes, yes. Just a dry throat is all." He composed himself, never wanting to show any frailty. He was still a strong man for his age and proud of the fact. Any sign of weakness was abhorrent to him.

"Can I get you some water?"

"I'm fine, Alexis. I'll just get something to drink when I get back to my office. I see you brought Harry some lunch." He pointed to the tray on the night stand.

"She did," Beest chimed in. "She's been babying me these past few days, Boss. I'm not used to that."

Wyld smiled and wrapped his arm around Alexis's shoulders. "Well, we just all want you to get better, my boy. Don't we, Alexis?"

"Of course, Father. Now I have to get back to my studies and Harry was about to wash up."

Alexis kissed her father on the cheek and then left the room with a quick backwards glance at Beest.

Damn, she's nothing but trouble. The words raced through his thoughts.

"So Harry," Wyld addressed him directly. "It appears you're healing quite well."

"Right, Boss." Harry touched the stitches still embedded at the top of his forehead. "And I'm going to have a beaut of a scar to prove it."

"Indeed. By now Big Swede knows it was us who put him in his place. I'm going to need you fit and ready should he try to come at us."

"Don't worry, Boss. I'm really okay. In fact, I think it's time I moved out of here and went back to my own place. I really don't like imposing on you like this."

"It's no problem, Harry. Why don't you wait until tomorrow? Stay another night. I sometimes feel the house is too big. It feels empty all the time, with just me and Alexis now."

Beest felt the conversation was moving along a strange path and he didn't know what to make of it. "Yeah, I suppose you're right, Boss."

Topper Wyld folded his hands behind his back and cocked his head slightly. "Harry, are you messing around with Alexis?"

"What? Hell, no, Boss…Mister Wyld."

"If you are, don't lie to me."

"I swear it, Boss. Sure, she and I flirt around a little, but that's all. Geez, Boss, I'd never do anything else."

"All right," the white haired father sighed. "Just remember, since her mother's passing, Alexis is all I have. And I want something else for her, Harry. Something more than this life of ours. That's why her education is so important and all."

Harry Beest didn't know what to say to that. Wisely he kept his mouth shut.

Shit, I don't need any of this now.

"You understand me, Harry?"

"Ah, right, sir. I do."

"Good, because if I ever discovered otherwise, it would hurt me greatly."

"Sure, Boss. Really, I would never touch her."

"Well, then," Wyld shrugged. "Guess I'm just being a doting father. You get back to your bath and lunch. I'll talk to you later."

Wyld patted Beest on the arm and left, closing the door behind him.

Beest stood looking at the door and swallowed.

"Damn."

The rest of the day was routine for Harry Beest and during his normal activities he found himself recalling what had happened between him and Alexis Wyld. He'd be conversing with Topper Wyld about future operations and find himself suddenly remembering the feel of her in his arms, the taste of her lips on his. Luckily these were only brief flashes and the Boss didn't notice.

Beest chided himself mentally for these lapses. He'd had so many women in his life, he had lost count. So why should one brief embrace and kiss bother him so much? He was starting to act like some lovesick Romeo. Alexis was no different then any other dame. He kept telling himself that and kept his focus on his present tasks.

He spent part of the afternoon at the guest house making sure the boys were all good and while there assigned Arnie Britwell the job of taking inventory on their supply of ammunition. They had fired a lot of rounds during the Cardigan raid and he wanted to make sure their stock was back to full capacity. At the same time he told Reed Vengel to clean the weapons used in that hit.

"Geez, Harry, can't that wait?" Vengel balked, sitting on a sofa in the main room, cleaning his fingernails with his jackknife. "I was hoping to get to the horse races later. I've got a couple of hot tips."

"Sure, after you clean the guns," Beest wouldn't budge. "Understood?"

Vengel's face turned sour. "Yeah, right. I hear ya."

Walking out of the house, Beest encountered Bruno St. George.

"How's the shoulder?" he inquired recalling the hit St. George had taken.

"Still a little stiff," the square-jawed St. George told him. "How's your head?"

Beest gently touched his stitches. "Better. At least the headaches are gone."

"How long you planning on staying in the big house?"

"Just tonight and then tomorrow I'm back here. So if you clowns are screwing off behind my back—"

"Ha, no way. Harry. Will be glad to have you back. None of these goons can play poker like you can."

"Say, where are Jack and Tommy? I didn't see them inside?"

St. George rolled his eyes. "Those two. Take a guess?"

Beest caught the look and grinned. "Madame Sadie's."

"Where else? Those two are the horniest fellas I've ever known."

"As long as they stay out of trouble," Beest pointed out. "The Boss doesn't mind if they blow off a little steam. With those two, you never know what's gonna happen."

"Amen to that, Harry."

"Okay, do me a favor, Bruno."

"What's that?"

"I told Revenge El to clean up the guns. Make sure he doesn't skip out before the job is done."

"Will do, Harry." At that, St. George entered the guest house and Harry Beest returned to the mansion. Dinner was only a few hours away and he had another meeting with Topper Wyld before then.

By the time Harry Beest climbed into bed at midnight, he was ready to close his eyes and forget the past day. Dinner had gone off as well as could be expected with Alexis sitting across from him acting completely unaffected as if their morning clutch hadn't even happened. She chatted about her current college courses with her father, made some comments about school friends and possible theater tickets to a new downtown musical etc. etc. etc. All the while Beest did his best to act normal and bored.

When the meal was over she departed, supposedly to do more school work while Beest accompanied Wyld back to his office for brandy and cigars. The Boss never seemed to tire and it was long after eleven when he finally decided to call it a day.

Beest had washed up, donned his pajama pants and made himself comfortable under the covers. He switched off the light, lay his head on his pillow and closed his eyes.

But sleep wouldn't come and though he was tired enough, all he did was toss and turn trying to find a decent relaxed position that would finally allow him to doze off.

Which is what was happening when the sound of the door opening snapped him alert. He reached out and switched on the table lamp.

Alexis, dressed in a black silk see-through nightgown was locking the door. "Alexis?" Beest sat up.

She approached the bed smiling. "Do we really need the light, Harry?" she teased, as her hands began to untie the black cord around her middle.

"What the hell do you think you're doing?"

"Oh, Harry, you know damn well what I'm doing."

"Stop it. We can't do this," he argued, doing his best to maintain his resolve.

"Then tell me to leave," she opened the negligee and let it drop to the floor. She stood naked before him, hands on her hips. "Go on, Harry, tell me to leave."

His heart began to beat faster. The sight of her was breathtaking, her body a gracefully sculpture model of feminine beauty from her elegantly shaped legs, to her tiny waist and full, round breasts. Her raven colored hair cascaded over her shoulders and her eyes were aflame with desire.

When he failed to answer, Alexis came over to the bed, sat on its edge and let his arms enfold her. As they kissed, he pulled her down and let his hands explore her hungrily. She sighed. He broke the kiss, reached up and once again put out the light.

Their lovemaking was a consuming fire neither could quench.

Somehow he knew it was the beginning of his doom but he didn't care.

CHAPTER (20)

The last thing Waldo Dunzinger ever expected was that he'd become attached to a wild, silverback gorilla. Yet that's exactly what had happened in the weeks since Korgo's arrival. Tasked with feeding the creature in its second floor cage and cleaning up after it, Waldo at first had been very weary. Knowing Korgo's violent history, he never stood too close to the iron bars and would merely toss in whatever was on the menu; be it bananas, vegetables or other assorted fruits. He'd learned early on, at Prof. Bugosi's tutelage, that gorillas were vegetarians and feeding Korgo any kind of meat would have only resulted in making the beast sick.

It was bad enough cleaning up his shit and piss, a task the diligent Waldo initially had thought would be impossible. Whereas the carnival people had left Korgo's steel manacle around one of his legs affixed to a six foot long chain. Waiting until the gorilla was asleep one night, Waldo snuck into the room and reaching through the bars, took hold of the chain and quietly pulled it through the bars. Then he wound it around two of the sturdy poles and clamped it together with a padlock he'd bought earlier at a nearby hardware store. Upon hearing the snap of the lock, Korgo had awakened and immediately rushed that side of the cage. Waldo barely managed to fall back from the beast's grasping hands.

He then turned on the lights, grabbed a mop and a bucket half filled with soapy water and brought them to the cage door. At this Korgo rushed at him only to be jerked to a halt by the chair. Furiously he tried to pull the chain free of the bars, but it was unbreakable and he could move no further. Seeing this, Waldo had quickly entered the cage and hurriedly mopped up the floor as best he could. Once done, he took the bucket to the washroom in the laboratory and dumped the filth down the wide circular drain. Returning to the cage, he used the wrung out mop to sweep the floor dry of any remaining water and then he was done.

After locking the door, he set down his cleaning implements and cautiously moved around the cage to where he had anchored Korgo's chain. The animal watched him with its small, beady eyes, its nostrils flaring in anger at having been thwarted in its rage to punish him. Now it glared at him.

"Okay, Korgo," Waldo reached into his back pocket and pulled out a fat, red apple. He held it out for Korgo to see as he neared the bars. Suddenly the gorilla lunged for him and he jumped back a step.

"No!" he said loudly. He waved the apple in front of the Korgo's face. "Be good...or no apple."

Again he reached forward with the tempting fruit. Korgo snorted, his arms still reaching out past the bars. Carefully Waldo brought the apple to one of those massive mitts and the gorilla grabbed it. The hairy thing fell back on its haunches, sniffed the apple and then took a bite devouring half of it.

"That's it," Waldo approved, nodding his head. "Be good and Waldo will take good care of you. I promise."

From that moment on, the disfigured servant and the gorilla developed a strange and unusual rapport. Korgo got used to Waldo's presence and accepted it. And the more Waldo brought him sweet treats, the more docile the silverback became. In whatever passed for its brain, Korgo came to understand the tall ugly human wasn't anything like his previous carnival tormentors.

One afternoon Prof. Bugosi walked in on Waldo as he was pouring fresh water from a can into Korgo's large water bowl. The animal stood a few feet away watching quietly. Then, when Waldo was finished, the gorilla came over, took hold of the bowl and raised it to its mouth.

"That's a good fella," Waldo complimented, holding the now empty can. "I'll bring you some fresh bananas later."

"I see the beast has taken a liking to you, Waldo," Bugosi said, as he came to stand by his tall servant.

"Yeah, Professor. He's really not a bad gorilla. I think those carnival people just treated him bad is all. That's why he fought them."

"Well, be that as it may, you shouldn't get too attached to it, my boy."

Waldo looked down at the scientist, a question in his eyes.

"He's an experiment, Waldo," Bugosi reminded him. "When the time comes, he will serve a greater purpose. You understand that, don't you?"

"I guess so, Professor. It's just that he's kind of nice now."

"Immaterial," Bugosi turned to leave. "All I require is his body when the time comes. Whether he is nice or not will have no bearing in that. Keep that in mind."

Bugosi closed the door behind him and Waldo looked at his new hairy friend with a feeling of utter sadness.

It just wasn't right. No matter what the professor said, Korgo was a good gorilla.

Mount Calvary was the final resting place of the Catholic parishioners who belonged to St. Michael's Church. Located on the eastern outskirts of Cape Noire, the fenced-in twenty acres was a bucolic setting where dirt roads crisscrossed manicured grass on which were rows and rows of tombstones. The landscape was a plateau of rolling hills on which with copse of trees from leafy oaks and elms to straight, heart pines dotted the scenery.

On this particular day, Detective Dan Rains stood alone on one such rise smoking a cigarette and witnessing the austere funeral of the Cardigan family. Two hundred yards below him three graves had been dug side by side. Two would receive the caskets containing Dick Cardigan and his wife while the third was prepared for the two smaller coffins containing their children.

Rains inhaled nicotine as he watched the cemetery crew with their heads bowed as Father Denis O'Malley, the pastor at St. Michael's, read from his bible. His deep voice carried and the detective easily recognized the words from psalms identifying God as the Good Shepherd.

It bothered him that no one had bothered to come to the funeral. Not one single person. Word on the street was that Topper Wyld had footed the expense for both the church service and this plot for the family's final resting place. Then again, Dick Cardigan had been a gangster and sealed his own fate the day he chose a life of crime and violence. Most of his so-called friends would know to stay away. In their eyes, the matter was finished and attending the funeral would only bring them to Wyld's attention. Which was to be avoided at all cost.

Rains blew out a cloud of gray smoke wondering at just how powerful fear could be. From his own short experience on the force, he'd come to sense that fear. It lived and breathed on every single street and corner of the city.

"In the name of the Father, Son and Holy Ghost," Father O'Malley finished making the sign of the cross over himself. It was the signal for the caretakers to start lowering the caskets.

O'Malley happened to look up and spotted Rains. The detective gave him a salute, tossed his cigarette and started back to where he had parked his car.

The city of fear had won again.

For the next two weeks things were quiet in Cape Noire. At least as quiet as they could be. Petty crimes and random homicides continued to flourish in the port metropolis which was more than enough to keep the Cape Noire PD busy morning, noon and night. What was blessedly absent was any major gang activity from either Topper Wyld's people or those employed by Big Swede Jorgensen.

Sometime after the Cardigan massacre, Fat Jacob Wiseman had been seen going back and forth between both mob bosses and it was generally assumed by the criminal underworld that he had brokered some kind of momentary truce between the rival outfits. Whether true or not, most folks appreciated the peace. Everyone was well aware it wouldn't last forever.

"Now what the hell is that?" Molly McCoy wanted to know as she watched her son-in-law, Butch Hammer, holding open the front door so that two men in coveralls could carefully maneuver an appliance of black steel into the Gridiron.

"What's it look like?" Butch fired back as the delivery men continued to wheel their heavy cargo around the bar's end and head into the kitchen.

Peggy Hammer stood behind her mother with little Rafe in her arms. The second the delivery truck had pulled up outside, she'd picked him up. It was the only way she could keep the rambunctious little waif from getting underfoot.

"It looks like a goddamn grill?" Molly blurted out, her voice betraying her own disbelief.

"Ma!" Peggy put a hand over Rafe's left ear. "I don't want Rafe hearing that kind of talk."

Molly shook her head. "Forgive me, child." Then she went over to the kitchen entry in time to see Butch directing the two men where to set the grill. It looked brand new and stood at the same height as their old stove. Butch had them slide it into the space to the stove's left side, after having them push the icebox away by a foot. The grill was soon snug between the two other appliances.

"You okay with plugging her in?" one of the haulers inquired.

"I got it," Butch replied.

"Good." The fellow pulled out a manifest sheet from his back pocket along with a pen. "Then sign this for me and she's all yours, Mr. Hammer."

Hammer opened the sheet, set it on the counter and hastily scribbled his signature on the bottom line. Done, he handed it and the pen back to the delivery man.

"Thanks, fellas."

"Our pleasure, Mr. Hammer." The fellow touched the brim of his wool cap and then he and his partner departed.

Molly stepped into the kitchen followed by Peggy still holding her son.

"So who's idea was this?" the old woman asked while eyeing the fancy new grill.

"It was ours," Peggy responded going to stand by her husband. "Butch thought it was time we started serving more than just cold sandwiches."

"Oh, you did, huh?" Molly ran a hand over the top of the grill. "And what exactly did you have it mind?"

"Hot dogs and burgers," Hammer told her happily. "And later, who knows. But for now we start with those two. I'm betting we'll sell lots of them."

"Well you'd better hope so," Molly finally resigned herself to the idea. "Cause it ain't gonna pay for itself until you do."

At that little Rafe laughed. "Hot dog. Me want a hot dog!"

Revenge El left the race track ripping up the tickets he'd bought that were guaranteed to give him a winner. All of them had been on losers. Not one of his five horses had even come in third and all he had to show for another wasted afternoon at the Downs was empty pockets. Digging into his jacket pocket he found four crumbled dollar bills. At least he'd be able to buy himself something to eat once he got back to the city.

He could have eaten with the other men in Topper Wyld's employ. Wyld always made sure his house Chef made extra for them in the guest house. But that would have meant putting up with everyone's razzing about his lack of skills when it came to picking winners. The little thug didn't need that aggravation on top of his own depressed mood.

He walked across the street from the track to the bus stop and sat on the bench along with two other losers by the looks of them. Hell, if anyone there had won big, they could have afforded to call a cab. Nah, the other two crestfallen guys looked as bad as he felt.

He pulled out his pack of Luckies, lit one up and then feeling generous, offered a smoke to his companions in misery. One said no, the other hastily took the free butt with a polite thanks. They were both halfway through their smoke when the big city bus rolled up three minutes later.

The driver opened the door and a few riders climbed out. Then Reed Vengel and the other two losers got on. The driver depressed the clutch, let off the brake and sent them rolling around the corner and headed back to Cape Noire. The Downs, as the track was called, for owner Charles W. Downs, was located southwest of the city.

As they were rolling along through early evening traffic, Vengel sat in the middle of the vehicle, looking out the window at the passing landscape and wondered which diner he was going to pick for supper. As he was pondering this question, the bus came to another corner adjacent to a busy intersection and Vengel looked up to see they were passing a small inn that catered to motorists. It had one main lodge for registration and to either side five small cabins for the customers.

It was still dusk and the light over the main office brightly lit the couple now emerging from within. There was something about the guy and the dame holding his arm. When the mousy crook recognized Harry Beest, he sat straight up in his seat. He pressed his nose against the window glass.

Who was that he was with? As she moved around Beest, Alexis Wyld came into view and Reed Vengel nearly choked. The Boss' daughter!

The bus lurched again and began to drive away from the motel, with Vengel craning his head around to watch as Harry Beest and Alexis Wyld made a beeline for the nearest cozy cottage.

He fell back against his seat still not believing what he'd just seen.

Harry and the Boss' girl.

Damn! That was hot stuff.

But just what was he going to do with it?

That was the question.

Tommy Bonello hated going out into the woods. He'd never cared much for the outdoors, especially after having lived on the streets of Cape Noire while growing up. At least in the city there was always some dumb drunk to roll, a vegetable stand to swipe an apple or an old lady to snatch a purse from. In other words, plenty of prey to hunt. Whereas, once you were in the woods, it was all nature and no victims. In fact, the forests on the outskirts of Cape Noire had their own predators like bobcats and bears and who knew what else?

No siree, Tommy Bonello preferred having concrete under his shoes and not be stepping in squushing pine cone needle mush. He hefted a shovel over his right shoulder as brother Jack half pushed and dragged their latest victim further into the gloomy green cathedral all around them. Early in their criminal education, Harry Beest had driven them out to the wilderness and educated them on the practicality of burying their bodies there far from prying eyes.

"Please don't kill me," the man with his hands tied behind his back pleaded. He was a fat little gent with a shiny bald head and large wire framed glasses over his gray eyes. Sweat beaded his brow and his double chin jiggled as he continued to beg for his life.

"All I did was skim a few grand. Really. That's all. I'll pay it back, I swear it."

His name was Carlton Petrie and he was one of Topper Wyld's accounting clerks at his trucking firm, Northern Van Lines. Wyld used the fleet of trucks to transport illegal goods and drugs over the Canadian border. Poor old Petrie had worked for him for six years. Then at Fat Jacob Wiseman's advice, Wyld had brought in an independent auditing firm to examine the company's books and it was then learned the sneaky little Petrie had been keeping two sets of books.

"Two hundred grand in the last year isn't what I'd call chump change,"

TOMMY BONELLO HATED GOING OUT INTO THE WOODS.

Jack Bonello argued as they came to a small clearing. It was late afternoon and the sunlight coming down through the canopy was beginning to wane. The area was one the twins had used often. "All right, far enough."

Petrie, breathing heavily, looked all around frantically. "No, please fellas. You can't do this. I got a wife and kid."

"You should have thought of that before you started dipping your fat little fingers into the till. Mr. Wyld gave you a cushy job and a decent pay. But you had to get greedy and see where it's gotten you."

Tommy Bonello dropped the steel tip of his shovel and shrugged. "Shut up, you little runt, and be grateful it'll be over quick without too much pain."

Petrie's eyes doubled in size as if he was just beginning to comprehend his predicament. Or what Tommy had just said.

So the killer clarified his statement. "It'll give you a little more time."

"Aaghhhh…" Petrie yelled and started to run away. He stumbled on an exposed root and fell to one knee. Panting, he rose up to continue his futile flight.

Jack Bonello pulled his .45 automatic from his shoulder holster and shot him in the back. The shot echoed through the trees and dozen of birds in the branches above took flight. Petrie cried out and fell to his face. Jack walked over to him and saw the wounded accountant was crying. He leaned down and shot him in the back of the head.

"Shit," he mumbled looking back toward Tommy still holding the shovel in his hands. "All right, you start digging and I'll finish it up."

Two hours later Tommy Bonello tapped the packed dirt over Carlton Petrie's unmarked grave as Jack sat with his back against a massive elm tree sipping from a steel flask. He removed his jacket and laid it across his knees. His shirt sleeves, like Tommy's, were rolled up to his elbows. Tommy walked over, laid the dirt digger against the bark and reached out for the small container. Jack handed it over and Tommy took a swig of the whiskey it held.

"Damn," he said, wiping his lips with the back of his hand. "Got to be a better way of burying folks."

"Well, we could always make them do it first before we shoot them," Jack suggested as he got to his feet.

"Hmm, that's not a bad idea," Tommy grinned handing back the flask. "Next time let's do that."

The twins started walking back to where they had parked their car.

"Been meaning to ask you, Jack. You notice anything strange about Harry lately?"

"Strange? How do you mean?"

"I don't know," Tommy hitched up his shoulders. "It's like his mind is always on something else. I think it might be a dame."

"Oh, yeah? What makes you say that?"

They had reached the sedan and both of them tossed their jackets into the back seat. Jack got behind the wheel and Tommy dropped into the passenger seat.

"Well, think about it," Tommy continued, as Jack started the engine. "When's the last time he went to Madame Sadie's?"

"Geez, I don't know." Jack looked over his shoulder as he carefully backed the auto through several trees and onto the dirt road. "A few weeks."

"Jack, it's been over a month. And the last time I even brought it up, he said he was busy."

"Busy? That doesn't make any sense."

"No, unless he's got a dame stashed away somewhere. One he doesn't want us to know about."

Twilight had fallen and Jack turned on the headlights. "Okay, so say you're right. Then why wouldn't he want us to know about her?"

"That's what I mean. Ain't that strange to you?"

"Yeah. It is, Tommy. Damn strange."

CHAPTER (21)

The second biggest room on the ground floor of Topper Wyld's mansion was located to the east side front corner; it was his war room. The main feature of the room was a long rectangular conference table, with six chairs to either side and one each to the facing ends. There was also a well-stocked bar and brick fireplace to keep both body and soul warm during winter sessions.

A week after Mr. Carlton Petrie's demise, Harry Beest was summoned into the war room and ordered to bring along Reed Vengel, Jack Bonello, and Bruno St. Martin. Tommy Bonello was out of town on a different assignment for the Boss. It was after dark and upon walking into the room, Beest saw Mr. Wyld was already entertaining his lawyer, Fat Jacob Wiseman who was seated in a specially crafted chair made of hardwood sipping a brandy. Wyld had been standing and when his men entered, he waved them to take their places at the table.

At the same time he told Reed Vengel to get them all a drink from the bar. The little rat-faced thug was familiar with what each of his pals enjoyed in the way of alcohol. He went to the bar and started mixing drinks.

"All right, gentlemen," Wyld wasted no time in getting the meeting under way. "It appears the heat has finally cooled off from the Cardigan raid and things are gradually starting to calm down.

"Wouldn't you agree, Jacob?"

"I would," the obese shyster lifted his shot glass to Harry Beest. "To a mission expertly executed, Mr. Beest."

Beest merely nodded.

Vengel came over with their drinks on an oblong steel tray and set it in the center of the table. Each of the gunsels reached out and took his own. St. Martin and Bonello had bottled beers, while Beest preferred a whiskey on the rocks like his Boss. Vengel's had mixed himself a Tom Collins.

"A toast," Wyld said, getting to his feet and raising his drink. "To a successful campaign!"

The others rose except for Fat Jacob. His bulk made such efforts last longer than was necessary and he knew Wyld never took any personal affront to his remaining seated.

After everyone had drunk, they sat again and Wyld began telling them what his plans were for the coming months. All of which will eventually lead to their doubling the size of their territory in the city. It was good news to all.

Still Beest was somewhat perplexed as to the reason for the gathering. He and the Boss had covered the same agenda not two days earlier. It wasn't like Mr. Wyld to waste time repeating things, even such crucial strategies. And why were the guys there? Sure, it was one thing to have St. Martin along. Bruno had been with the gang for a few years. Jack was still wet-behind the ears and Vengel was a nobody; an errand boy at best.

None of it made sense. He felt as if the room was getting hot and loosened his tie.

"Something wrong, Harry?" Wyld stopped what he was saying and eyed him strangely.

"Ah...I feel hot all of a sudden, Mr. Wyl—" Pain shot through Beest' abdomen and he doubled over. "Aghh."

Everyone in the room was startled. Everyone but Topper Wyld.

"What's the matter, Harry? You don't look so good."

Beest grimaced as the pain intensified. "It hurts...bad."

Harry Beest began to convulse wildly and fell out of the chair onto the floor where he continued to twist about wildly. St. Martin and Bonello began to get out of their chairs to go to his assistance only to have Wyld stop them.

"Don't any of you move!" He commanded. "Stay right where you are."

It was at that moment the hall door opened and in walked Professor Bugosi and his assistant, Waldo. Bugosi had on his gray topcoat and matching homburg along with his soft kid gloves.

"Ah, right on time, Professor." Wyld smirked and pointed to the man on the floor. "Your patient is ready for you."

Bugosi stepped around the table and looked down at Beest. His gyrations had stopped and he appeared to be comatose. The dark-haired scientist looked to his giant aid. "Be careful with him, Waldo."

"Yes, Professor." The brutish Dunzinger went down on one knee, scooped up Harry Beest in his arms and picked him up as if he were a child.

Bugosi and Wyld shook hands. "I will let you know when the operation is completed," the happy Hungarian immigrant smiled. "Thank you for such a wonderful specimen."

With that he exited the room followed by Waldo carrying the unconscious Harry Beest.

Once gone, Wyld turned his attention to his now puzzled audience. All of them were too scared to say anything out of line. Still not certain what exactly it was they had witnessed. Wyld took a deep breath and sat motioning for them to do so as well.

Reed Vengel sat nervously hoping none of the others would ever learn that it was he who had poisoned Beest's drink with something the Boss had given to him earlier in the afternoon. Even now, he felt a bit uneasy being the one who betrayed Beest, but hey, this was a dog-eat-dog business. Too bad for Harry. But he wouldn't ever be pushing Revenge El around again.

"Jack," Wyld addressed his young ward.

"Yes, Mr. Wyld."

"You are now in charge, Jack. Don't disappoint me."

Upstairs, Alexis Wyld was studying when she heard the sound of a car engine pull up in the back yard. It shut off and she merely assumed it was some of her father's men arriving late for his conference. Ten minutes later she heard that engine start up again. Curious, she put her notes down and walked to one of her windows.

She peeled back her curtain in time to see a long black limousine drive off. In the glow of the compound's lamplights, she thought she recognized her father's weird associate, the one called Prof. Bugosi.

A shudder passed through her. There was something sick about the man that gave her the willies. She let the curtain fall and went back to her studying, putting the incident out of her mind.

The darkness that had enveloped Harry Beest gradually began to lift as he regained consciousness. As his awareness returned, he was aware of being on his back and—for whatever reason—totally immobile. He blinked his eyes several times against a bright light beating down on him. When he'd opened them fully, he discovered he was strapped to a table in Prof. Bugosi's laboratory; a place he'd been many times with Boss Wyld.

"What the hell!" he blurted out and tried to raise his head only to discover he couldn't do it.

"Ah, you're awake," Prof. Bugosi appeared from behind him, looking down at him. "Don't waste your time in attempting to move, Mr. Beest. I've injected you with a chemical that has paralyzed your nervous system."

Sure enough, the madman was telling the truth. Beest couldn't move any of his limbs. It was as if he was a lifeless mannequin on that table.

"But why?" he shouted, unable to control his frustration.

"Please, no need to be so loud," Bugosi came around to his left side and patted him on the shoulder. Beest realized the scientist was decked out in a white surgical gown with matching rubber gloves. Both of which were smeared with a dark red substance he suspected was blood. "I don't know why you fell into disfavor with Mr. Wyld as that doesn't concern me, sir.

"My only concern is that we are about to make scientific history, Mr. Beest. You and I are about to expand the borders of human knowledge."

"Huh, what are talking about?"

Rather than answer his captive directly, Bugosi motioned with his hands to someone beyond Beest's view. "We are ready, Waldo. Push that table closer.

His eyes straining to see past the professor, Beest saw Bugosi's man, Waldo, come into view pushing another table closer to his own. On it was the body of what appeared to be a large, hairy gorilla. Prof. Bugosi stepped back so that Waldo could set the second table within two feet of the first.

Now Beest could see the top of the gorilla's skull had been removed. Dried blood and bits of gore were congealed around the cavity's edges. Then he remembered something the Boss had told him weeks earlier. About Bugosi wanting to put the brain of a man in the body of gorilla.

NO! Beest's sanity threatened to escape his reason. *He can't do that! It's impossible!*

"Stop, please. What are you going to do? Tell me!"

Bugosi stood next to the lifeless simian and rubbed his gloved hands together. "Isn't it a marvelous creature, Mr. Beest." Bugosi smiled broadly as he realized his own pun. "My, my, one beast to another. How poetic."

"That's crazy, you can't do that. No one can. You'll only kill me."

"Oh, let's hope not, Mr. Beest. I mean, poor Korgo here gave his life for science. Can we do any less?"

Bugosi stepped out of Beest's line of vision going to a table where his surgical tools were set. But Beest could still hear him.

"All right, Waldo. It's time for the gas."

"Yes, Professor."

More noises. Then the twisted face of Dunzinger was standing over Beest with a black rubber mouth piece. As he brought it down, Beest could smell the chloroform and tried to hold his breath. Waldo clamped the device over his mouth and Beest began to inhale the knock-out gas into his lungs.

"That's it," Prof. Bugosi was back beside him. In his hands he held as small electric saw. "Just close your eyes and go to sleep, Mr. Beest."

The world began to spin for Harry Beest.

He could hear someone laughing and then a loud buzzing sound coming closer and closer.

Then there was only blackness again.

Alexis Wyld came downstairs and found her father in his office already on his second cup of coffee and working over a set of papers on his desk.

"Ah, good morning, Alexis," he smiled looking up at her in the doorway. "You just getting up?"

"Yes. I don't have any classes this morning. My first isn't until one this afternoon. I was hoping maybe Harry could drive me to school."

"Ah, I'm afraid Harry's on an errand for me, sweetheart. He won't be back until some time tomorrow."

"Oh." She kept the expression on her face neutral. "I see. Well, maybe one of—"

"I'll have Tommy drive you. All right?"

"Of course, Father." She stood looking at him feeling a sense of unease. Something was wrong, but she didn't know what it was.

"Is there anything else, dear?"

"No, I guess I'll go have some breakfast."

"Do that. Chef Louis whipped up some excellent blueberry pancakes this morning."

"Sounds yummy." She gave him a little wave. "Later."

As she walked away, Topper Wyld wondered what her reaction would be when next she saw her lover. He hoped it would be a lesson his daughter would never forget.

A typical Pacific Autumn fog had crept over the docks of Old Town by mid-afternoon and the Rolls Royce Silver Ghost moved along the narrow docks like its namesake. A purring engine accompanied the sleek gray outline. Reaching its destination, the rich automobile came to a halt across the street from the Gridiron Saloon.

"It's pretty much as I remember it," Big Swede Jorgenson said, looking through the back window. Betty One-Eye sat beside him and Eli St. John was behind the wheel letting the motor idle.

"Oh, it's the same greasy spoon," the redhead concurred placing a hand on Jorgenson's knee. "But keep watching. The traffic is only going to get heavier and by evening the joint is mobbed."

Jorgenson could see the usual patrons; the sailors, dock hands, and whores, going in and out at a steady clip giving proof to his lover's claim. "So what the increase in business? Is that woman McCoy still running the place?"

"She's still there, but she's no longer the owner. Several years ago she sold the place to her bartender, an ex-boxer from back east named Butch Hammer. He married her daughter, Peggy, and began making changes. Adding more dishes to the menu and generally sprucing the place up as you see it now."

Jorgenson put his own hand over Betty's and turned to her. "You really think it's worth my time?"

"I do," she nodded. "Never mind the paltry take it brings it, what I'm getting at is it could be a drop-zone for whatever junk you got coming in from the docks. A place to dump drugs fast before the cops or port authority even had a chance to inspect newly arriving cargo ships."

Jorgenson looked back at the diner and reflected on Betty One-Eye's concept. It had potential.

"All right, I like the idea. Offer them twice the going price for the place."

"And if they don't want to sell?"

"Then show them what will happen if they refuse your offer. Just don't make a public spectacle like you did with the pool hall. Wait until no one is around. Make it clear to them no one is to know about our new arrangement."

"Got it, Boss."

As St. John put the Rolls in gear and pulled away, Betty anticipated the fun she was going to have taking the Gridiron from that old hag and her family. It was going to be a pleasure.

It was the stench of dirty wet hair, musky and foul, that he inhaled that awoke Harry Beest. There were no lights and he was still on his back. But not on a table. He tried to rise up and confirmed he was definitely stretched out on a floor. A hard tile floor. His hands pushed down and felt the wrongness of it; as if everything in his body was foreign. He kept pushing until he was sitting up straight. Gradually his eyes made out shapes in the darkness. Bars. He was in a cage.

A cage?

He brought his left hand up before his face and it wasn't his hand. It was a gnarled, heavy appendage with thick black fingers, the knuckles fat with calluses. Immediately he raised the right one and it only matched the appearance of the left.

He was again repelled by the awful smell that wrinkled his nose. Even that action felt wrong. Carefully he brought those alien hands to his face and felt its contour. It wasn't his face! There were lumps, and grooves that felt like multiple gouges cut into his skin which was as tough as leather.

His jaw was longer with rough hair and his nose almost twice its size... and flat!

Panic flooded him. He couldn't think clearly. His ears picked up footsteps and then a door opened and light filtered in. There was a click and the room was fully lit from several overhead ceiling lights. He had to blink away their harsh white glare.

"Ah, awake at last," Prof. Bugosi said, as he entered the room and approached the cage. No longer in his operating scrubs, he was once again wearing a fancy charcoal gray three-piece suit. In his hands he held a clipboard and was making quick notes as he studied his captive. "How do you feel, Mr. Beest?"

"Arrrr..." the growl came out of Beest's throat and he tried again. "I... rrr...I..."

"Go slowly," Bugosi cautioned him like a benevolent doctor. "Your animal vocal chords don't work exactly as your old ones did. They will take some getting used to."

"Wha...arrr..." Beest attempted to get to his feet, which was when he looked down and saw how misshapen they were and covered entirely with black coarse hair. He almost fell over, his body wasn't the same. He grabbed for the bars to steady himself.

Beest snorted and forced himself to utter, "Wha...ddd...you...do...to... me?"

Bugusi didn't answer. Instead he walked over to a small wooden work bench set in a corner behind the cage. Hanging over it against the wall was a ten by eight mirror with a few cracks in it. The scientist lifted the mirror from its hook, turned and went back to face his now anxious patient.

Standing only a few feet from the bars, Bugosi help up the mirror in order to reflect Harry Beest's image.

And there it was. Beest pressed his face between two cold bars and looked at the reflection of a brutish, male silverback gorilla. As his eyes widened glaring back at him, a primal scream ripped from his fang adorned mouth. "NOOOOOOOOOOOO!"

Violently he shook the bars causing the entire cage to shudder.

"I'm afraid all your shouting and protestations will not change the facts, Mr. Beest. You inhabit the body of a healthy, vibrant African gorilla. Though I would caution you to try and remain a bit calmer as you don't want to tear the stitches holding your skull cap on."

Amidst his violent physical reaction to his plight, Beest looked closer into the mirror for the first time realizing the top of his head...his gorilla head…was wrapped in surgical bandages. He reached out with his right hand and touched them cautiously. It was all true, every insane bit of it.

I'm an animal!

"That's better," Bugosi nodded seeing Beest cease his tantrum. "I'm sure, after a while, you'll learn to adjust to your …ah…new persona."

"Grr…my…bdd…body…where…" Beest's throat was trying to carefully shape the words. As Bugosi had already informed him, his gorilla larynx and mouth had not been shaped to speak a human language.

"Oh, it's gone," Bugosi replied, casually. "Mr. Wyld instructed that it be destroyed after the operation. I had my man, Waldo, cut it into pieces and burn it in the cellar furnace. All that remains is ashes and pieces of bone."

Beest's entire body seem to deflate and the finality of what the mad man had told him ended any and all hope he could ever have of returning to a normal existence. Still holding the bars, he slid down to sit on his butt, his head bowed.

"My, my, you seem to accept defeat without question, Mr. Beest. I'm surprised. I thought a gentlemen of your past renown would see beyond such a one note predicament."

Beest was beyond caring what Bugosi was prattling on about and didn't even bother to raise his head.

The scientist continued. "The point you are failing to grasp, sir, is this. What I can do one time, I can do repeatedly."

The gorilla's head looked up.

"Just because your body has been cremated does not mean I can't put that brain of yours into another at any time I choose to do so."

The implication of that statement was beginning to burgeon fully in Beest's mind when Bugosi's servant, Waldo, walked into the room, purposely avoiding looking at Beest. He was still sad at the loss of Korgo. The gorilla's brain had gone into the fire along with the gangster's corpse.

"They are here," he reported.

"Good," Bugosi handed Waldo the mirror. "Put this away and then go show them up. We mustn't keep Mr. Wyld and his daughter waiting."

At the mention Alexis Wyld, Beest's attention returned. Grasping the bars tightly, he pulled himself back to his feet. It felt awkward. The urge to fall over on to his hands was powerful, but he wouldn't give in to it. He wanted to stand like a man, not some jungle beast.

"No," he barked roughly.

"No what?" Bugosi cocked his head quizzically.

Beest waved his hand at the mocking scientist. "No…grrrl."

"Ah, you don't want Miss Wyld to see you in your new body. I'm afraid that is out of my control, sir. In this matter, Mr. Wyld is my employer. It was his money that paid for all my research and equipment. I can't deny him the satisfaction of seeing the result of his patronage."

Beest shook his head. Bugosi only chuckled. He was enjoying himself and Beest wished for a second he could get his new massive hands around the twisted genius' neck.

"In here," Waldo Dunzinger's voice was heard. A second later the door opened and he ushered in Topper Wyld and his beautiful daughter. Wyld was as ever attired in a stylish, tailor-cut suit, topcoat and hatless. Alexis, on his arm, wore a heavy cotton blue coat with a white fur collar over her knee length yellow dress, a matching blue cloche and white satin gloves.

Coming up behind them alongside Waldo, was the diminutive little Reed Vengel, his newsboy cap in his hands.

"Father, why are we here?" Alexis inquired looking about the room.

"Why to see Harry, of course," Wyld replied. "He's been the Professor's guest these past few days."

Nervously Alexis looked at Bugosi and then the cage and its occupant. "But there's no one else here?"

"That's not quite true, Miss Wyld," Bugosi made a sweeping gesture with his hand towards the big silverback gorilla behind him. "I believe you do know this particular ape and he you."

Alexis addressed her father. "What does he mean, Father? I don't understand?"

"Look at it, my dear." Wyld removed her hands from his arm. "Take a closer look. I'm sure you'll recognize your paramour; though he has a changed quite a bit since your last romantic rendezvous."

Confused, Alexis Wyld once again looked at the caged animal. She began to move closer and Bugosi stepped out of her way, still smiling deviously.

For his part, Harry Beest's torture was unbearable. Seeing the woman he loved before him. Her fear and puzzlement. He felt his heart being torn apart.

"AA...LEX...IS!" he cried out.

She froze in mid-step. Hearing her name from the gorilla's mouth shocked her. Her breath caught and she stood mesmerized. She looked at the brutish bestial features and then the marble-like black eyes. They were wet with tears.

And then she knew.

"Harry?"

The crying gorilla's head fell in utter defeat.

Alexis' fist came to her mouth. "No...no! It can't be!" She whirled on her father. Topper Wyld held his head high not deeming to say a word. She knew the truth of it. Without another word, she screamed and fled the room.

Wyld looked back at Vengel. "Go see her to the car. I'll be along shortly."

"Yes, sir," Vengel wasted no time rushing out of the room. The sight of the caged gorilla had spooked him. Especially when it had spoken Miss Alexis' name. But his mind refused to believe what the girl had so readily accepted.

Having achieved what he desired, Topper Wyld went to stand next to Bugosi and speak to his former lieutenant.

"I warned you, Harry," he began, his hands behind his back. "I told you in no uncertain terms to stay away from my daughter. But you just wouldn't listen, would you? Well then, here we are."

Beest merely glared at him, breathing heavily.

"Oh, I'm sure you'd love to hurt me now, wouldn't you, Harry?" Wyld surmised, a cruel smile on his face. "But I want you to keep two things in that stupid mind of yours. One, I could just have easily had you killed and we wouldn't be having this conversation."

"Though I seem to be doing most of the talking."

Wyld held up his right hand, two fingers extended. "No, I don't want you dead. That would have been too easy. I want you to remember this for as long as you live. I've told the Professor to release you later, after I'm gone..."

"Grrr...killll...uuu," Beest managed.

"No, Harry. Because my second point is; even if you should manage to survive out there in your new body, should you ever attempt to harm either myself or the Professor, then you will seal your own fate. As I'm sure he has told you, it is within his power to repeat this procedure and put that idiot brain of yours back into another human body."

Wyld leaned closer to the bars. "Do you understand me, Harry! Hurt either me or Bugosi and you will stay trapped in that freakish body 'til the day you do die. And I'm sure it is a day you will come to wish for often.

"Do I make myself clear?"

For a second the gorilla Beest only stared at his former boss, then slowly he nodded his head in defeat.

"Good, then we understand each other." Wyld faced Bugosi. "I don't care where you dump him. Perhaps the alleys of Old Town. I leave that to your discretion."

"Of course, Mr. Wyld," Bugosi was only too happy to obey. "And my new funds?"

"I'll deposit another check in your account tomorrow morning. Good night, Doctor."

"Good night, Mr. Wyld. As ever a pleasure working with you, sir."

After Topper Wyld had departed, Professor Bugosi gave Waldo his orders, making sure Beest heard every word.

"Do as Mr. Wyld, suggested, Waldo and take Mr. Beest in the truck and take him to the harbor docks. There you will release him."

"Yes, sir." Waldo lived to serve his master.

Bugosi then spoke to Beest. "I trust you remember what Mr. Wyld said and not give Waldo a hard time. It would be pointless, Mr. Beest. As of now, your fate is once again back in your hands."

He didn't expect the gorilla-man to comment and he was right.

Harry Beest merely stood in silence. Whatever that fate was, he had no choice but to accept it.

Once inside their Cadillac, neither Topper Wyld or his daughter said a word and both remained silent for the entire ride back to their home. Upon pulling up to the front entrance, Alexis jumped out of the back seat, bolted up the stairs and into the house before Reed Vengel could come around to open the door for them.

He stood there nervously as Topper Wyld climbed out and adjusted his coat lapels. He looked at the open door and then back to his rat-faced driver.

"Return the car to the garage. I won't be needing your services the remainder of the night."

"Right, Boss."

Wyld stood scrutinizing Vengel. As much as he'd appreciated the weasel's betrayal of Beest, he also despised his spineless character. He'd known too many selfish bastards like Vengel during the early days of his criminal career. Men who would sell out their own mothers to further their own ends.

"You are not say a word about what you saw tonight," Wyld commanded.

"No, sir. I swear, not a peep."

"Then go. Get out of my sight."

"Yes, sir, Mr. Wyld."

Revenge El hurried back into the driver's seat and steered the big auto around the building to the garages in the back yard.

Topper Wyld looked up at the starry sky and sighed. It was time to face his daughter's wrath.

Inside the main room he was greeted by Frank Channing, his chief of security. There were always four men on duty inside the mansion at all times. Channing, a stocky-built forty-year-old of British descent, reported everything was quiet; the chef and cleaning staff having retired to their rooms hours earlier. Wyld told him he'd most likely be in his office working late and did not want to be disturbed. Channing would relay that directive to the other three guards.

This done, Topper Wyld started up the stairs to the second floor. He went to his own bedroom first to divest himself of his hat and topcoat and then went to the other end of the hall and knocked on Alexis' door.

There was no response.

"Alexis," he spoke through the door. "Let me talk to you. Please. I can explain."

When she failed to reply, he grabbed the knob, pulled the door open and entered. His daughter was stretched out on her bed, her sobbing face buried in her pillow.

"Go away!" She lifted her head; her cheeks wet with fresh tears. "I hate you."

"You don't mean that. You're upset now. In time you'll come to understand what I had done was for the best."

At that Alexis sat up and jumped to her feet, her hands balled up in fists as she screamed at her father. "How could you do...that...to Harry! I loved him!"

Wyld refused to be baited and stood calmly, his hands at his sides. "Alexis, you're only eighteen. You're still a child."

"No, I'm a woman. Harry's woman. And now you took him away from me."

Wyld smirked. "What, you think because you had sex, that makes you an adult? My dear Alexis, please listen to me. You may have been in love with Harry, but that's a far cry from true love.

"Never mind the fact that the object of your affection could never have stayed faithful to you. Surely you must know that?"

"Harry loved me. I know he did."

"Alexis, Harry only ever loved himself. It was only a matter of time before he tired of you and started frequenting his favorite cathouses again. It was just his nature."

"I don't believe it," Alexis stamped her foot.

Topper Wyld reached out and took hold of her shoulders, his face softening. "He wasn't good enough for you, my dear. That's why I did what I did. Don't you understand? In time, I am going to be the most powerful man in Cape Noire.

"I am building an empire, Alexis. One I hope to leave to you one day. But before that can happen, you have to grow up. You have to finish your education and begin taking your rightful place at my side."

"What, and be alone like you are?" She sniffled.

"No," he corrected her. "One day I do want you to marry, but someone worthy of you and your place in the scheme of things. A doctor or a lawyer, someone with a rich family and name in this town."

"Do you really mean that, Father?"

"Of course I do, my dear." Wyld pulled his silk handkerchief from his breast pocket and handed it to her. "Now you dry your eyes and try to get a good night's sleep. You'll see. Things will look a whole lot better in the morning."

He reached out and kissed her forehead before leaving her alone.

Alexis fell back on her bed and wiped her face with the monogrammed handkerchief. All she could see in her mind was the gorilla in that cage.

"Poor, Harry," she said to herself. "What are you going to do now?"

Harry Beest was bounced around like a loose rubber ball in the back of the empty box truck. He had been herded into it by Bugosi's man, Waldo Dunzinger, who had used an old baseball bat to move him along. At the same time the brute had kept Beest's feet shackled together by the three foot chain and steel manacles clasped around his feet. Even in his current state of despair and confusion, he knew any attempt to escape thus fettered would have been ridiculous.

Even if he could run, where the hell would he run to?

Climbing into the truck, Beest had sensed the hour was late. Maybe

EVEN IF HE COULD RUN, WHERE THE HELL WOULD HE RUN TO?

it was after midnight now and during the ride, he'd not heard much traffic through the truck's walls confirming his assumption. The way the unbalanced vehicle swerved from right to left every few minutes, he could imagine the narrow streets of Old Town and all the imposing rows of warehouses that filled several blocks facing the docks.

After about a half-hour, he felt the truck slowing down and the driver down-shifting. They came to an abrupt stop and once again he was roughly tossed onto his side. Whatever shocks the truck had once been outfitted with had long since worn out. As he turned his new body around to get into a sitting position, the back door was raised up and Waldo Dunzinger stood there, a queer expression on his face. Behind him were darkened piers and the outlines of massive cargo ships at anchor in the harbor.

"Push your legs closer," Dunzinger said, holding up a key so Beest could see it. "And I'll get those chains off you."

The gorilla/man scooted over using his hands and Waldo unlocked both manacles. He opened them and lifted them off Beest's feet before stepping aside and indicating the ground before them. "Come on, get out. You're free to go."

Beest dropped the three feet to the hard pavement and almost fell on his face. He couldn't quite stand straight and let his new arms support him. No wonder his knuckles were so big. This was how gorillas got around, hunched over, using both their hands and feet to move. He'd seen that in several jungle movies.

"Go on," Waldo said. "Get out of here."

Harry Beest snorted and again tried to form words. "Thrr…anks."

"Yeah, right." Dunzinger pulled down the door, secured it and started back to the cab. "Good luck, Korgo."

He started the engine and the truck lurched forward, turned to the right and vanished into one of the alleyways between two massive warehouses.

Harry Beest scratched his face. *Who the hell is Korgo?*

Looking around, he felt exposed being out in the open. He began lumbering down the road, his hands and feet moving in unison. It was a strange rhythm but felt right and allowed him to move at a fast and easy clip.

At one point he came upon several derelicts gathered around a drum fire passing around a bottle of wine. He approached them directly hoping they might be able to help him. But when one of the drunks saw him emerge from the darkness, he screamed, "AAEEE…A MONSTER!"

The man and his mates started running away as fast as their legs could carry them. In his haste, the one with the bottle dropped it without a second thought.

Beest watched them flee and feared this would be his fate from now on. Who in their right mind would help him, a jungle gorilla loose on the streets of Cape Noire?

Somehow the wine bottle hadn't broken on impact and was a few feet in front of him; some its contents spilling out. The gorilla Beest picked it up, sniffed the top and then tilting his head back, took a long swallow. It was a hardy red and warmed his belly. He finished what remained and then tossed the bottle away. This time it did smash loudly against the road.

He shrugged and started shambling down the street again.

CHAPTER (22)

Butch Hammer finished mopping the floor and lifted his apron skirt up to wipe his face. He reached over to finish the glass of beer on the bar that he had been sipping on as he'd pushed the wet mop back and forth across the dirty tiles of the saloon's floor. Draining the beer, he noted the circular clock hung over the door to the kitchen indicated it was almost 1:20 a.m.

No wonder he was tired. It had been a long day and he couldn't wait to put the cleaning stuff away, shut off the lights and get upstairs where his family was sound asleep. Tomorrow would be another day.

He had just started to roll the bucket filled with soapy water behind the bar when there was a loud banging on the front door. Hammer looked up and could see a couple of figures through the glass top of the door.

Now who the hell was that? He moved closer to door and called out, "Go away! We're closed!"

This only elicited more banging from his unwanted guests. If they kept it up they'd wake Peggy, as the ceiling wasn't all that sound proof and noise did carry upstairs. And it wasn't only Peggy they would arouse, but also little Rafe. Angrily he marched to the front door.

"I said, we're closed!" he repeated.

Arriving at the front entrance, he was surprised to see standing there none other than Betty One-Eye and her herculean black companion, the one called Eli St. John.

"Let us in," the tall redhead demanded.

"No," he shook his head. "It's after one, come back—"

Betty lifted up her right hand and showed him the .45 automatic she was holding. She pointed it at him. "Open the damn door or die," she said clearly enough. "Now."

Hammer wasn't one to be threatened easily but he'd heard enough about the one-eyed bitch in the past to know she would do it. Betty One-Eye's reputation was that of a stone-cold killer.

Hammer fumbled reaching into his pants pocket, found his set of keys and unlocked the door. He took several steps backward letting the woman and her mean-looking pal enter. The gun in her hand never waivered.

Betty One-Eye had on her usual attire of black pants and shirt under her wrinkled gray unbuttoned trench coat. On her feet were a pair of heavy scuffed work boots and black leather gloves covered her hands. Her trademark red tresses dangled in a long ponytail down her backside. St. John had on jeans, a short waisted jacket and an old moth-eaten baseball cap whose bill he kept pulled down over his eyes.

"What do you want?" Hammer queried. "If it's to rob the place, you're going to be sorely disappointed. We ain't got more than a few hundred in the register."

"I didn't come here to rob you, Butch," Betty-One grinned. "In fact I'm here to give money. Lots of it." With her empty hand, she reached into the topcoat and withdrew a folded piece of paper which she then slapped onto the bar.

"What's that?" Hammer had no clue what was happening.

"It's a bill of sale," Betty One-Eye explained. "You see, Butch, Big Swede wants to buy this joint of yours and he's willing to pay three times what its worth."

"Huh? Why? What's this place to him?"

"Let's just say he thinks its worth something to him and leave it at that."

Hammer knew he was in a bad position. Facing two cold-blooded killers with only a mop in his hands. Still, the Gridiron Saloon was all he and Peggy had. Were he to give it up, he had no idea where they would go? What they would do? No matter how good the offer was, this old dive was their home; theirs and Molly McCoy's.

"Sorry, but no thanks," he finally said. "I'm not selling."

"Aw," Betty One-Eye frowned. "I was hoping you wouldn't make the mistake of thinking you had a choice."

She twisted around and shot the long mirror behind the bar. The gunshot was deafening only to be followed by the shattering of the mirror as hundreds of pieces showered the floor.

"Shit!" Hammer cursed.

"Understand now?" the redhead asked, turning the gun back on him. "You sign this paper or—"

Her second shot took out the front plate glass window. In an instant cool night air came sweeping into the bar.

"All right, stop it!" Hammer dropped the mop and raised both his hands. "Enough…no more. I'll sign it."

"I thought you'd see the light," Betty smiled. She pointed to the paper with her pistol and Hammer walked over to pick it up. He unfolded it and gave it a cursory glance. It didn't matter what it said, he already knew that.

"You got a pen?"

As Jorgenson's lover pulled out a pen from her coat pocket, Hammer thought he heard noise from above. It has to be Peggy. The shots would have done it. All he wanted to do now was sign the damn paper and get the two mobsters out of the place before his wife made it downstairs. He knew once he put his name on the document, there was nothing stopping the patch-wearing Betty from shooting him on the spot.

Clutching the pen, he started to lean over the bar.

Then all of them heard a savage roar from outside.

As Eli St. John began turning around, a massive furry shape came flying through the busted bay window at him. Its vicious mouth opened wide in a beastly cry, fangs exposed. St. John's eyes registered the giant gorilla falling on him and terror clutched his heart just before two powerful fists beat down on him. Both fists connected with St. John's chest and drove him to the floor, stunned.

Harry Beest then jumped up and down on the gunman caving in his chest. St. John's mouth opened and blood gushed out like a fountain.

Betty One-Eye stood frozen, unable to move. The gorilla smashed his foot down on her ally's head and it was flattened like a melon.

She screamed. Harry Beest looked at her and shook his new gorilla body. He'd recognized both Betty and St. John upon coming to investigate the gunshots. He didn't know why they were terrorizing the bartender but none of that mattered to him. All that mattered was he finally had an outlet for the fury boiling up inside of him. And so he'd attacked.

For Betty One-Eye, seeing the nightmarish animal destroy St. John brought back a long ago warning from the voodoo women in Little

Jamaica. "Beware the monkey man."

The gorilla roared again and with two steps fell upon her before she could even raise her gun. It forcefully took hold of her head and lifted her off the floor with it. Betty tried to bring up her automatic.

Hammer, a shocked witness, heard a second scream and turned to see his wife, Peggy, rushing to him from the back door dressed in her robe. He caught her in his arms and together they watched as the gorilla twisted the one-eyed Betty's head, snapping her neck as if it were a dry twig. Her entire body went limp in death.

Peggy buried her face in Butch's chest as the silverback then tossed the lifeless body onto one of the booth tables. Beest stood breathing hard; his naked gray chest heaving in and out. Then, as he began to relax, the gorilla dropped back to its knuckles.

Butch Hammer hugged Peggy wondering if they would be next.

The gorilla approached them slowly, snorting. It's small round eyes boring into Hammer's.

Then it said in a rough but quiet voice, "Help me."

Fat Jacob Wiseman was an insomniac; a condition that had come about due to his all-night study sessions while in law school. Later, long after having earned his degree and begun his practice in Cape Noire, he'd discovered sleep had become an elusive prize he rarely could attain. In the end, he merely accepted the fact that most nights would be spent in his den either reading, his one true passion, or listening to big band music from the local radio station.

Thus, he was seated comfortably on his favorite chair, a glass of brandy on the end table by his side and a lit cigar in his mouth when he heard a knocking at his front door at three o'clock in the morning.

At first he thought he'd merely imagined the sound but then it was repeated, distinct and sharp.

"Hmm," he mumbled, placing the bookmarker before closing the book and setting it on the table. With a mighty heave, he pushed his big body off the chair and then cinched his robe's belt tighter around his middle. Keeping the cigar in his mouth, he walked into the hall and toward the house's open vestibule.

Wiseman could have used the intercom on his desk to page his chauffeur,

Andrew Cornwell who lived in a small apartment above the connecting garage where his modified hearse was kept. But for the moment he saw no need to disturb the man as he didn't sense any real threat—as yet.

He was almost at the door when there was another knock. Wiseman flicked on the outdoor light. "Hold on, I'm coming."

He carefully unlocked the bolt but kept the chain in place. Considering his line of employment and the pedigree of his clients, he was always cautious. Even though he'd worked at remaining a neutral agent in the city's criminal community, one could never be too careful. Which is why as he pulled back the door with his left hand, his right went into his robe pocket and took hold of the small two-shot derringer he kept there.

"Who's there and what do you want?" he asked looking through the small gap. The man facing him under the overhead lamp was a complete stranger.

"Ah, sorry to disturb you, Mr. Wiseman," the fellow said. He looked to be in his forties, rugged with a two-day old shadow on his jaw and hatless. "My name's Butch Hammer. I own the Gridiron Saloon down in Old Town." The man was obviously nervous and fidgeting.

"I've heard of it," Wiseman acknowledged. "Why are you here, at this late hour, Mr. Hammer?" Wiseman could see over his visitor's shoulder at a parked Ford pick-up truck at the front curb. His home was a two story Cape Cod House situated at the end of a cul-de-sac.

"Ah...Harry Beest asked me to bring him here."

"Harry Beest?" Wiseman didn't seen anyone before him except Hammer.

"Yes, sir. He's in...ah...some trouble."

"Trouble? What kind of trouble."

Hammer raised his right hand. "Please, sir. Don't be scared. Okay?"

"Scared?"

It was then that another figured stepped up from the side where it had remained hidden from view to stand next to Hammer.

Fat Jacob Wiseman gasped. It was a real live gorilla.

It looked straight at him and then said, "Wiseman, it's me, Harry."

"Harry! But...."

"I know," Beest continued. "Please, I need your help. Let us in. I promise, we won't hurt you. You have my word. Please."

Wiseman was totally amazed. He also had very few choices before him. Either shut the door on this talking gorilla and find himself waking up in his chair, the victim of a truly bizarre dream. Or open the door and let them in.

It was his curiosity that won out.

"All right," he agreed, closing the door to undo the chain link.

He flung the door open and ushered them in. "Let's go into my den down the hall to the right."

"Ah, thanks, sir," Hammer stayed put by the still open door. "But I think this is as far as I go with all this."

Fat Jacob looked between his two visitors. The gorilla Beest nodded at Hammer and brought up his huge hand.

"Thank you," he said, as Hammer shook hands with him.

"No, Harry, it was you who saved me and my family," Hammer reminded Beest. "I owe you, fella. You ever need anything, all you got to do is ask. Good luck."

Harry Beest and Fat Jacob Wiseman watched Butch Hammer leave, closing the door behind him. Then Wiseman pointed down the hall.

"Now, Harry, let's get settle in and you can tell me what happened to you. I've a feeling it's a story like none I've heard before."

Forty minutes later, Harry Beest, seated on the reinforced sofa in Fat Jacob's den, concluded his story about how he'd run afoul of Topper Wyld's wrath and become an experimental guinea pig for the mad Professor Bugosi.

"And here I am," he concluded with a loud burp. Almost lost in his hand was an empty bottle of beer; the third such Wiseman had provided him with from his kitchen icebox.

"Dear God in heaven," the attorney commented. "That's by far the wildest thing I've ever heard in my entire life." He was back in his comfort chair sipping on another brandy. "In fact, if you weren't sitting right here in front of me right now, I'd never believe it. It's just too incredible."

"Yeah, tell me something I don't know already."

"But what about your own body, Harry? Where is that?"

"Wyld had Bugosi burned it. Give it to the Boss, he don't miss a trick. As of right now, I'm stuck in this…this body and I can't lay a hand on either him or that wacko, Bugosi, 'cause if I do, there goes any chance I ever have of being a human again."

"I understand. You're right, Topper is holding all the cards. Damn it, Harry, I'm truly sorry this happened to you. But why did you have Hammer bring you here? How can I help you?"

"Look, I'm not out of the game yet. I got at least three hundred thousand dollars stashed away in a safety deposit bank account at the First National. I'm was hoping you can get it for me. Act like my lawyer, if you will."

Wiseman emptied his glass and smacked his lips. "Mmm, all right. I see what you are getting at. Acting as your agent, I can withdraw those funds, either all or whatever you need. I'd recommend not emptying out the account. You're going to need a place to live, Harry."

"Right, and that ain't about to be a cage in the zoo."

"No, of course not. In fact, I've a few friends in real estate who just might be able to set you up with a nice, fancy place only a few blocks from here."

Beest was nodding. "Yeah. Now you're talking. That's why I came to you, Wiseman. I figured if anyone could help me now, it would be you."

"Okay, I'll take you on as a client. But for now we have to keep this really hush-hush."

"You worried what will happen if Wyld finds out?"

"No. Oh sure, I figure he'll be upset, but considering what you did to Big Swede's people at that bar, I think I can smooth over his ruffled feathers and convince him having you around is still a good thing for him."

"If you can do that, you're a bloody genius, my friend."

"Nothing's impossible, Harry. I've learned that over the years. It's how you approach a problem that determines the outcome."

Fat Jacob Wiseman clapped his hands together. "You've given me an exciting new challenge, Harry. But before we do anything else, I am going to have to introduce you to my talented friend, Guiseppe Manora."

"Who the hell is that?"

"You'll see, Harry. Oh yes, you'll see."

CHAPTER (23)

It was after lunch when the call came into the precinct in regards to a woman's body found floating in the harbor down in Old Town. Lt. Clement Serat took one of the station squad cars and drove out there hoping it would just be some down-on-her-luck nameless whore who'd decided to end it all. Such suicides were common enough and if it was a Jane Doe he'd get away with a whole lot less paperwork.

As he came onto the main boulevard facing the harbor, he rolled past the Gridiron Saloon and saw the owner, Butch Hammer, standing on a ladder out front nailing a huge piece of plywood in front of what was obviously a smashed plate glass window. That was noteworthy, but then again not overly so. Mostly likely the damage was due to a bunch of rowdy sailors causing a ruckus. The joint was noted for its rough and tumble patrons. Sailors, especially the foreigners, were always trouble.

Still, it was strange he hadn't heard anyone at the station house mention anything about a disturbance the night before. Hell, he shrugged behind the wheel, if no one had called it in, it was none of his concern.

Up ahead he saw a small crowd gathered by a long fisherman's pier where an ambulance had backed up to the end of the dock. Several boys in blue were standing around a body hidden under a white sheet.

Serat parked behind the crowd of onlookers, stepped out of his car and took his pack of Lucky Strikes out of his coat pocket. He lit one up and inhaled deeply. The air was cool and the smell of sea salt prevalent. Overhead noisy gulls circled as if also curious as to what was going on. Serat took another drag and then pushing his way through the gathering, started walking to the crime scene.

Dr. Art Sippo was already standing up and making notes in his small notebook. Three of the uniformed officers greeted Serat, including Sergeant Paul Malloy who happened to be the senior man on the spot.

"Okay, Malloy, what do we have here?"

"Lieutenant," the half-black/half Chinese veteran greeted. "A couple of fellas coming in from doing some deep-sea fishing, spotted the body just outside the breakwater about to get washed away with the tide. They hauled her on board and brought her back here."

"Yay, lucky us," Serat replied, sarcastically blowing out more cigarette smoke. "So where are they now?"

Sgt. Malloy pointed to the edge of the dock, over which Serat could see a single mast jutting up. "Still anchored there. I told them they'd need to give you a statement."

"Okay. Look, why don't you go ahead and do that while I talk with the doc here and we'll see about getting an I.D."

"Sure, Lieutenant. No problem."

As Malloy went to the pier ladder and started to climb down to the small fishing boat, Serat went over to Dr. Sippo.

"Afternoon, Doc."

"Lt. Serat." Sippo pointed to the sheet covered body. "You got a murder on your hands."

"Ah, hell. And why is that?"

"She didn't drown. She was dead way before being dumped in the drink."

"How?"

"Something…or someone broke her neck?"

"Any identification on the body?"

"I was just about to do that. Though that's your job, not mine."

"I know, don't remind me."

"Want to see her?" Sippo lowered himself to one knee and reached for the nearest corner of the sheet.

"Yeah, why the hell not. Go ahead."

Sippo pulled the sheet away and Lt. Clement Serat immediately saw the leather eye patch over the woman's left eye. And he knew.

"Goddamn it!" he cursed. It was going to be a long, long day.

At the same time Lt. Serat was wondering how he was going to handle the death of Big Swede Jorgenson's female killer, an old convertible DeSoto was rocking to a clacking stop in front of Fat Jacob's home. In the front seat were Mr. Guiseppe Manora and his wife of thirty years, Alphonsa. Both were Italian immigrants who had come to America in their teens and settled in Cape Noire to make their fortune.

As Mr. Manora climbed out of the front seat, he twisted his plump body around and grabbed the leather case on the back seat. Mrs. Alphonsa, almost twice his size, was huffing and puffing as she made her way around the back of the auto.

"I dunno comprende," she mouthed while waving her heavy arms about. "You make a Mr. Jacob brand new suits and pants only last week. Why now he wants more?"

"Hush you mouth, Mama," Mr. Manora warned her as they started up the steps to the front door. "Is not for us to tell Mr. Jacob when to buy his clothes. If he wants more coats and pants, I'mma only too glad to make them. He pays so good. We dunno have our business without him."

As he finished his last entreaty, he knocked on the door.

Jacob Wiseman appeared a second later and waved them in with a friendly smile.

"Ah, Guiseppe and Mama Manora, thank you for coming on such short notice."

"Issa fine, Mr. Jacob," Mr. Manora said happily, as he and his wife followed their rich client into his ornate den. "Any time you want us, Mr.

Jacob. We come."

"Well, that's so gracious of you. I do have an emergency on my hands."

"How so, Mr. Jacob? You need more fine suits?"

"Oh, no, it's not for me. You see, one of my associates recently fell on hard times and was left…well, how can I say this. He has no clothes at all."

Guiseppe's face scrunched up. "No clothes?"

"Naked as a jaybird, I'm afraid."

"That issa bad."

"Indeed it is. We need you and your wife to make him an entire new wardrobe. Everything from formal wear, to every day outfits. You see, my associate is rather a large fellow, ah, like myself."

"That no problemo, Mr. Jacob. We happily make clothes for your friend."

"Excellent." Wiseman clapped his hands. "He's in the kitchen. Let me call him in." The Lawyer then went to the hall door and called out. "Harry, would you come in here please. My tailor and his wife have arrived."

There was the sound of footsteps and then Harry Beest stepped into the den.

Mrs. Manora screamed and fainted on the spot.

Mr. Manora gulped hard and then uttered, "Mama mia!"

It was long after business hours when Big Swede Jorgenson entered the City Morgue located in the basement of City Hall. Billy Miser, the clerk on the night shift was on Big Swede's payroll and, upon learning the identity of the newly registered murder victim, had gone to a nearby drugstore phone booth to call the mob boss. Now Miser admitted Jorgensen and two of his men through the back door next to the loading dock in the back of the building.

He led Jorgenson to the embalming room and there the somber, weary gangboss ordered his bodyguards to remain in the corridor and make sure no one disturbed him. Once inside the main room, Miser switched on the overhead florescent lights and led Jorgenson to the wall of stacked drawers. He went to the middle drawer in the center row and pulled it out to reveal a corpse wrapped in a dark green canvas body bag.

Miser started to unzip the bag but Jorgenson stopped him. "I'll do that. Now leave me alone with her." The tone in Jorgenson's voice was emotionless and Miser, a sniveling opportunist, knew enough not to oppose his orders.

He bowed slightly and left the room without another word.

Big Swede pulled down the zipper and tugged the sides apart to expose Betty Ann McCauley's face. It was bloated from her time in the water and tilted at an angle where the neck had been broken. Her skin was a pasty white and she looked like a life-size doll. Her good eye was thankfully shut. Had it been opened, he would have lost whatever composure he now maintained.

Men like Big Swede didn't love. It was beyond them. They only possessed and in that regard he mourned Betty's loss. That she had been taken from him. Looking down at her he still had trouble believing she had finally met her match. He'd almost come to think of her as invincible. Of all the killers he'd employed over the years, none had been more efficient than Betty. She loved her job and did it well. It was perhaps the only thing that ever gave her real pleasure. She really was a sadistic, heartless bitch.

But who could have done this? Certainly not that bartender, Hammer. It was inconceivable that he alone could take down both Betty One-Eye and Eli St. John. Which brought the second mystery to mind. Where had St. John disappeared to? Was he still alive or had he also met the same end as the redhead?

Questions piled up on one another. Including the most important. Who had done this?

He sighed. It had to be Topper Wyld. No one else would have the balls. And coming on the heels of the Cardigan fiasco, it seemed like Wyld was sending him a second warning. It was the only thing that made any sense.

He could retaliate. But not having concrete answers, he'd be doing so based on a guess and that could be a serious mistake. One with lasting consequences. No, for the time being, he would have to accept that trying to grab the Gridiron had proven a critical error and cost him too dearly. For now, he would leave it alone. Best to let the dust settle and then see what transpired in the months ahead.

Maybe Wyld would tip his own hand. For now that was all Big Swede could hope for.

He touched Betty's cheek gently. "So long baby, it was fun. Give the Devil my regards." He re-zipped the bag and then walked away. Miser could close things up.

Big Swede was just too tired and he sorely needed to rest.

"I can't believe this!" Topper Wyld shouted at Fat Jacob Wiseman. "What on earth possessed you to help him! After everything I did to destroy him?"

Their heated confrontation was taking place in Wyld's office, two weeks after the events in Professor Bugosi's laboratory; the last time Wyld had seen Harry Beest.

"Which was a somewhat rash decision on your part," Wiseman retorted calmly. He was seated on the big chair in front of Wyld's desk. Off to the side Jack Bonello stood with his arms folded across his chest trying to make sense out of what was being said. He had no clue. He too had been wondering what has had happened to Beest since he'd collapsed at the strategy session and been carried away by that mad doctor and his lumbering stooge, Waldo. Wyld had never mentioned his lieutenant again since that evening and Bonello had wisely avoided the subject. Truth was, he was getting to like being the Boss' new number one guy.

"Oh, and now you're correcting me, Jacob?" Wyld's face had turned red upon hearing Wiseman's account of how he'd come to Harry Beest's aid. Wiseman had left nothing out in his report from helping Beest access his bank funds to helping him purchase an expensive house in the Heights, the ritzy section of Cape Noire. But there was one part of the story he had purposely omitted until he felt the moment was right to use it.

"You know very well, that is not my intent, Mr. Wyld." Wiseman pursed his lips and proceeded to reveal his ace card. "On the night he was changed, your man Beest came across two of Big Swede's henchmen attempting to threaten the owners of the Old Town bar, the Gridiron Saloon."

"So?" That tidbit had derailed Wyld's anger. "What's that got to do with me?"

"Everything, sir. You see, Big Swede had sent them there to take over the establishment. Much as he'd done with Saul Chevesky Pool Parlor five years ago."

"What?" Wyld turned and looked to Jack Bonello. "Why wasn't I informed of this, Jack?"

"Ah...because I'm just hearing about this now like you are, Boss."

Wyld returned his attention to Fat Jacob. "So, what happened?"

For the first time since arriving, Wiseman smiled. "Jack never heard about it, Mr. Wyld because the attempt failed. You see, Beest, in his new ...ah...shape, came across the scene and intervened. He killed both of Big Swede's people and with the help of the bar's owner, tossed their bodies into the harbor."

"Sonofabitch," Wyld sat back in his chair. "Do you know which of Big

Swede's goons they were?"

"Indeed," Wiseman knew he had Wyld's interest now. "None other than Betty One-Eye and her assistant, Eli St. John."

"Holy shit!" Jack Bonello exclaimed. "She is...ah...was, one of the toughest guns in Cape Noire. Everyone knows that."

"Not anymore," Wiseman added. "Thanks to Harry. Don't you see, Mr. Wyld. Beest's continued presence among the gangs is the perfect foil between Big Swede's reckless ambition and your own strategies for the future. With him preoccupying Swede's actions, it leaves you free to plan and make whatever moves necessary without drawing any undue attention."

Topper Wyld drummed the fingers of his right hand on his desk. It was a habit he fell into when mulling over important issues. After a few minutes he, too, smiled.

"He really took out Betty One-Eye, eh?"

"Yes, sir. In fact a few of my contacts report seeing Big Swede at the morgue the night her body washed up."

Wyld began rubbing his hands together. "Ha, that serves the bastard right. He just never learns."

"So," Wiseman prompted. "Are you willing to leave Beest alone?"

"Yes, as long as his activities don't conflict with my own. That big gorilla can do whatever he likes. And good luck to him. I'm through with him personally. See that he understands that, Jacob."

"Consider it done, sir."

"Good, now who wants a drink?"

Fat Jacob Wiseman raised his hand.

The black Studebaker drove down the beautifully landscaped neighborhood the next morning carrying three men who were not at all comfortable in that section of Cape Noire.

"Are you sure this is the right address?" Arnie Britwell questioned from the back seat. Up front Baldy Dave Jackman held the steering wheel while Bruno St. George rode shotgun.

"It's what that Wiseman dude gave me," St. George replied. He held up the small sheet of paper in his hand. "See, I even wrote it down. This is the street and the house we want is number eight-forty-two."

"Then that's it over there," Jackman interrupted nodding his head to the old white mansion coming up on their right. A long circular driveway brought them to the front entrance shaded by a small portico.

"You have got to be kidding," St. George whistled. "Ain't no way Harry would end up living in a joint like this."

"Well, we're here." Baldy Dave shrugged. "Might as well go in and see for ourselves." He shut off the engine and started to climb out.

"You think there's any truth to that story Revenge El told us?" Britwell asked, coming out of the back. "You know, about Harry now being a gorilla and all?"

"Don't be freakin' stupid," snapped St. George angrily. "You know El is a bald-faced liar. He just made all that up to scare us. He never liked Harry and now that the Bone Brothers are running the show, he's a happy camper."

"Yeah, well I'm glad someone is," Jackman started up the steps. "'Cause I sure as hell ain't. Harry Beest is my boss and if he's starting up a crew, I'm in."

The other two nodded in agreement.

Upon reaching the door, they saw it was ajar. Then a voice called out from inside.

"Come on in, boys. I'm in the living room to the right."

St. George went first. The interior hallway was plush, with a carpeted staircase rising to the second floor. Before it was the opening to the main living room. They all entered together and there encountered the new Harry Beest.

The gorilla wore an expensive blue gabardine suit with a white shirt and maroon tie. On his big feet were the largest custom made leather shoes any of them had ever seen. And on Harry's head was a high crown dark gray fedora. In his mouth was a lit cigar.

Harry Beest, the gorilla mobster, took the stogie out of his mouth and said, "Welcome to my new home, fellas. What do you say we show this town what a real gang is all about? You boys with me?"

EPILOGUE

Countess Selena spread out her Tarot cards on her round table and began to decipher her first reading of the day. Three incense candles burned in the middle of the table sending a sweet smell throughout the room.

As she began to touch the various cards and deduce what their positioning implied, she noticed the center candle's smoke trail was beginning to take on the shape of a face. She stopped her reading and eyed the wispy image of Eli St. John.

"Eli? Is that you, boy?"

The face just looked back at her in sadness. Then it spoke with a soft ethereal voice.

"Tell my Mama...I is sorry. I is sorry."

The face vanished and Countess Selena crossed herself. Her only thought: *This is Cape Noire.*

THE END OF THE BEGINNING

ABOUT OUR CREATORS

WRITER

RON FORTIER – Comics and pulps writer/editor is best known for his work on the Green Hornet comic series and Terminator – Burning Earth with Alex Ross. He won the Pulp Factory Award for Best Pulp Short Story of 2011 for "Vengeance Is Mine," which appeared in Moonstone's *The Avenger – Justice Inc.* and in 2012 for "The Ghoul," from the anthology *Monster Aces*. He is the Managing Editor of Airship 27 Productions, a leading New Pulp Fiction publisher and writes the continuing adventures of both his own character, Brother Bones – the Undead Avenger and the classic pulp hero, Captain Hazzard – Champion of Justice.

In 2017, he was awarded the first, Pulp Grand Master by the Pulp Factory.

Fortier also writes the highly popular Pulp Fiction Reviews blog.

You can find him at (www.Airship27.com)

He created and continues to write the following independent comic book series; *Mr. Jigsaw Man of a Thousand Parts, Airship 27 presents All-Star Pulp Comics* and *Ron Fortier's Tales of the Macabre.*

ARTIST

ROB DAVIS - began his professional art career illustrating role-playing games in the late 1980s. Not long after he began lettering and inking, then penciling comics for a number of small black and white comics publishers—most notably for Eternity Comics, precursor of Malibu Comics, in the 1990s. He was penciller on their book SCIMIDAR with writer R.A. Jones. Finding work at other black and white publishers Rob eventually began working at both DC and Marvel. Rob worked on likeness-intensive comics like TV shows QUANTUM LEAP and STAR TREK's many incarnations, mostly on the DEEP SPACE NINE comics for Malibu. At Marvel he worked on the Saturday morning cartoon comic PIRATES OF DARK WATER. After the comics industry implosion in the late 1990s

172

Rob picked up work on video games, advertising illustration and Tee-shirt design as well as some small press comics like ROBYN OF SHERWOOD for Caliber. Rob continues to do the occasional self-published comic book and is publisher and designer for his small-press production REDBUD STUDIO COMICS. Rob is Art Director, Designer and Illustrator for the New Pulp production outfit AIRSHIP 27 partnered with writer/editor Ron Fortier. Rob is a two-time recipient of the PULP FACTORY AWARD for "Best Interior Illustrations" since 2010 for his work on SHERLOCK HOLMES: CONSULTING DETECTIVE and has been nominated for the same award many times since. He works and lives in central Missouri with his wife and two adult children.

robmdavis.com

What's come before...

WELCOME TO CAPE NOIRE

Located on the Northwest Coast, Cape Noire is a booming econommic giant whose inner core has been corrupted by all manner of evil. From the sadistic mob bosses who ruthlessly control vast criminal empires to the fiendish creatures that haunt its maze of back alleys, Cape Noire is a modern Babylon of sin and depravity.

Amidst this den of iniquity strides a macabre warrior committed to avenging the innocent and holding back the tide of villainy. He is *Brother Bones, the Undead Avenger* and there is no other like him. A one-time heartless killer, he is now the spirit of vengeance trapped in an undying body. He is the unrelenting sword of justice as meted out by his twin .45. automatics

His face, hidden forever behind an ivory white skull mask, is the entrance to madness for those unfortunate enough to behold it. These three previous volumes feature fast-paced, action-packed stories starring pulp fiction's most original hero, Bother Bones, battling the forces of evil in Cape Noire!

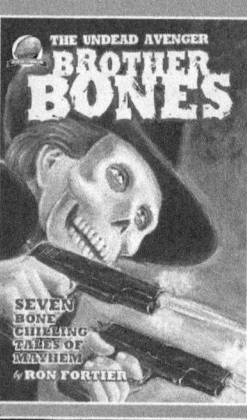

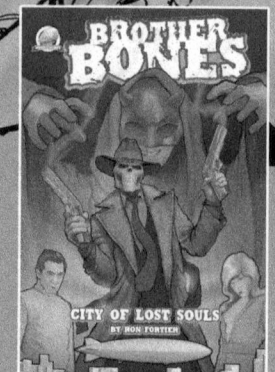

PULP FICTION FOR A NEW GENERATION!

FOR AVAILABILITY OF THESE AND OTHER FINE PULP STYLE PUBLICATIONS VISIT: AIRSHIP27HANGAR.COM

www.ingramcontent.com/pod-product-compliance
Lightning Source LLC
Chambersburg PA
CBHW051127260626
47170CB00005B/1696